PULL
A PUSH NOVELLA

NYLA K.

Copyright © 2022 Nyla K.
All rights reserved.

Paperback ISBN: 978-1-7359162-5-5

Pull is the intellectual property of Nyla K.

Except permitted under the U.S. Copyright Act of 1976, no part of this publication may be reproduced, distributed, or transmitted in any form or by any means, or stored in a database or retrieval system without prior written permission of the author.

This book is a work of fiction. Any references to historical events, popular culture, corporations, real people, or real places are used fictitiously. Other names, characters, places, and events are products of the author's imagination, and any resemblance to actual events or places or persons living or dead is entirely coincidental.

Cover Design: Moonshine Creations
Formatting: Moonshine Creations

BLURB

So you fell in love with your daughter's boyfriend?

What happens next?

I'll tell you... You finally begin to *live* again.

You take trips, celebrate anniversaries, and attend your first Pride parade as an out-and-proud polyamorous *throuple*, apparently.

Life isn't perfect for you now that you've had a brand new happily ever after. In fact, far from it. But you make it work. You find your way through the jealousy and the unrest of people who don't understand your quirky little family.

And most importantly, you *love*. You love so hard there's no possible way only one partner could handle it all.

It's a damn blessing I found two.

This book is dedicated to all the *PUSH*ers out there!

You have truly made my dreams come true.

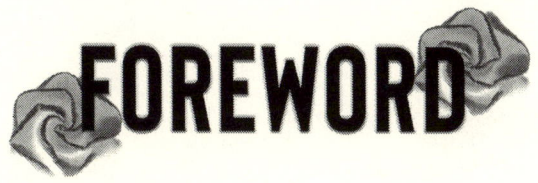

FOREWORD

This edition of *Pull, A Push Novella*, includes three bonus scenes that fill in some of the gaps from the *Push* storyline.

Then it includes *Pull*, the Pride novella from summer 2021.

And at the end, you'll find a new, surprise bonus scene!

Enjoy ;)

Please be advised that reading this novella before Push will sincerely spoil the story. You must read Push first before reading this conclusion.

PUSH PLAYLIST

With a few new songs added for PULL
Listen now on Spotify!

Jump – Julia Michaels
Beautiful (feat. Camila Cabello) – Bazzi
Lucky Strike – Troye Sivan
Love Lies – Khalid & Normani
Mr. Brightside – The Killers
Delicate – Taylor Swift
Glass House – Morgan Saint
Beast of Burden – The Rolling Stones
YOUTH – Troye Sivan
bad guy – Billie Eilish
Don't Stop Me Now – Queen
Ghosts (Stripped) – Scavenger Hunt
Without Me – Halsey
Slow Dancing in a Burning Room (Acoustic) – John Mayer
LOVE FT. ZACARI – Kendrick Lamar
Lights Down Low – MAX
Better – Khalid
Sit Next to Me – Foster The People
Bad Moon Rising – Creedence Clearwater Revival

True Love Way – Kings of Leon
Somebody Else – The 1975
Habits (Stay High) – Tove Lo
I Guess That's Why They Call It The Blues – Alessia Cara
lovely – Billie Eilish & Khalid
Everything Will Be Alright – The Killers
Hide and Seek – Imogen Heap
This Feeling – The Chainsmokers feat. Kelsea Ballerini
Jump (Acoustic) – Julia Michaels
Born This Way – Lady Gaga
no tears left to cry – Ariana Grande
Animal – Troye Sivan
Kiss Me More – Doja Cat feat. SZA
Love In This Club – Usher feat. Young Jeezy
Easy – Troye Sivan

PUSH
BONUS SCENES

The *Pain* of losing him,
The *Love* of getting him back,
&
The *Pleasure* of happily ever after times *three*.

RYAN
Christmas Eve Night

We walked into the apartment side-by-side. Silent.

Neither of us had said a word since we got into the car, and I supposed it would stay that way.

All the drama of the night must have taken away our ability to small talk.

It certainly sobered me up a bit...

And clearly the same could be said for Tate.

He was almost eerily quiet. I could feel the mood-shift radiating off of him, and it was making me tense. I felt guilty, for dragging him into my problems. He got punched in the face repeatedly tonight, because of me.

I felt like a piece of shit, and amongst all the other crap going on in my life, this was really weighing me down.

I left the Lockwoods' home feeling determined. I knew what I had to do, and starting tomorrow, everything was going to change in a monumental way. My head was spinning, and I felt outside myself.

Tate sauntered toward his bedroom and I followed him, slowly; hesitantly. I wasn't sure if he wanted me near him after what happened. But I was far too drunk to drive all the way home, especially at this hour.

I stood in the doorway, uncertainty rippling inside me as I watched him strip out of his clothes. He got down to his boxers, his movements heavy with what seemed like defeat.

I'm such a fucking asshole... I can't believe I did this to him.

Tate was a good guy. Sure, he could be overly narcissistic at times, and I didn't doubt that he had been purposely pushing Ben's buttons to get a rise out of him for his own bizarre amusement. But still. He didn't deserve to be beaten over the likes of me.

"I could... go..." I stuttered, my brow furrowing as I stared at his back.

He paused and glanced at me over his shoulder, exhaling a strong breath.

"Just... Get in bed. Please," he mumbled, then climbed into his bed, slinking beneath the covers.

Swallowing hard, I undressed down to my boxers, flipping off the light and making my way over to the bed. I crawled in, on the opposite side, resting my head on the pillow and closing my eyes. I wanted so badly to fall asleep; to decompress from all the insanity of the past month.

But the longer I lied in that bed, in the dark silence, the more I realized my brain wasn't going to turn off. There was too much happening in my mind. Too many thoughts, images and memories rushing behind my eyes.

Before I knew it, hours had passed—according to the clock on the nightstand—with no sign of slumber.

I tilted my head in Tate's direction. It was very dark, and I could barely see him, but I assumed he was sleeping. He'd been silent, just quietly breathing the whole time.

My mind began to drift some more, wondering what Ben and Jessica were doing. They were probably in bed, too. But Ben didn't sleep. Maybe he was awake at that moment... Thinking about me.

But I shook those thoughts away. *It's over. The sooner you forget about them and move on, the better.*

Suddenly, I felt Tate's hand graze my hip, and I froze. So he *was* awake.

His fingers ran across my stomach. I knew what he was doing, but I just couldn't bring myself to go there. After everything that happened tonight... with Ben... There was no way I could even think about messing around with Tate right then. My heart wouldn't have been in it at all, even though it rarely was with him, which made me feel like such a huge scumbag. Still, I had to figure Tate was alright with my distance. He'd picked up on it after that very first time, in the bathroom at that sleazy bar.

Tate scooted closer to me, trailing his fingers below my waist as his lips found my neck. He planted some very soft kisses along my flesh and I closed my eyes, seeing nothing other than Ben's face before I left his house.

He had looked so devastated. So somber and full of rage; confused, and hopeless. I missed him so badly already, and I knew it would only get worse from there.

I'm never going to see him again.

"Tate... I can't..." I whispered in the dark, remaining still.

His movements paused. "You're in love with him."

My chest tightened and burned, unwelcome tears fighting against my eye sockets.

Tate let out a soft breath on my neck, then lifted his head before mine.

"What does it feel like...?" he murmured, quiet, almost inaudible. I frowned up at his shadowed face.

It feels like fucking Hell, Tate. It feels like death a thousand times over, being in love with someone you can't have.

My body reacted on its own to the sadness and guilt, and I grabbed his jaw, pulling his lips to mine. He gasped, mainly out of surprise, but partly because I forgot his lip was cut open. I could already taste the blood...

But I didn't care. I kissed him harder, because I had to. Because he was *here*, and I needed it. I needed his body, in that moment, to distract me from my broken heart, still struggling to keep beating.

Rolling on top of him, I pinned him to the mattress, sucking his lip and touching his tongue with mine. I ground my hips into his, feeling him harden beneath me.

We said nothing more. I didn't answer his question, because I *couldn't*. We just kept kissing and touching. I turned my brain off and allowed the lust to fuel me; the desire to be with the man I loved, who wasn't there.

It was horrible, and I felt awful inside. But I needed something. I needed to *feel*.

Flipping Tate forcefully onto his stomach, I yanked his boxers down his legs while he pressed his hips up to meet my erection. He was panting; so obviously wanting me to fuck him, and erase the memories of what happened tonight. The fucked-up mess we'd caused together...

My lips brushed the nape of his neck while I removed my Calvins, kicking them away before spreading his legs with my knee. Growling and gasping, my movements were almost frantic in my attempt to prove I was fine. I don't think I was fooling anyone.

Tate squirmed away for a moment, and came back to me with a condom and some lube, which I wasted absolutely no time tearing open and sliding onto my cock. I squeezed out some lubrication and coated myself, gliding my wet fingers between his cheeks.

"Fuck..." he hummed, bending at the knees.

I stared down at his body for a moment. It was very dark in

his room, but not nearly as dark as it would have needed to be for me to think he was someone else.

My throat constricted. *He's not Ben.*

I rumbled to myself and closed my eyes, shaking my head as I spread him open and probed his hole with the tip of my dick.

This isn't what you want.

I pushed more, breaking into him slowly while he moaned my name.

It's not him.

"Fuck me..." he breathed, lifting his hips higher, forcing me in deeper.

Shoving my aching cock further into his ass, it throbbed at the tightness, and how fucking wrong it was, what I was doing. It felt wonderful and terrible all in the same.

My movements picked up as I thrust into him, pulling out and pushing back in, fucking him slow and deep. I gripped the sheets in my fist as I pumped my cock in and out, my balls meeting his.

In that moment, I was a machine, driven strictly by urges and the want to forget. I was so emotionally detached I barely even recognized myself.

"Is this how you fuck him?" Tate's brusque voice crept up to me and I groaned out loud, grabbing his ass hard. "Is this how it feels to be him...?"

Biting down hard on my lip, my tempo slowed. I imagined Ben's big, hard, perfect fucking body under me, writhing around in his need for me. His perfect ass, his smooth skin; how delicious he tasted.

I wanted him so bad, and I couldn't fucking have him, *ever*, the thought of which made me nauseous. But I was also screwing at the moment, my dick buried inside something, stroking, which did feel excellent.

There was a war going on between my brain, my heart and my body. And none of them had the slightest clue who was winning.

"I know you love him, Ryan..." Tate gasped while I pounded into him, slowly yet so deep and hard that his bed was shaking.

"Fuck..." I choked out a sob, chomping on my lip again for fear I would cry out Ben's name.

I wanted to say it so bad. I knew it was wrong... But God dammit... I wanted *him*.

I wished it was him beneath me. That was the problem. All I wanted in the world was Ben's love, and I couldn't fucking have it.

I was desperate, needy, and retching in despair.

Pressing myself down on Tate's body, I thrusted harder, holding onto him as I burrowed my face in his neck. He had a great smell... But still, it was so obviously not Ben's, it tore my heart apart.

Be him. Please... Please just be Ben.

I stifled a strangled noise, shoving Tate into the mattress as I chased my orgasm.

I love him. I want him. I need him.

He's. Not. Here.

"Ryan..." Tate rasped then moaned with the obvious pleasure he was feeling from my dick lancing his pleasure spot. "It's okay."

I whimpered and shook my head, licking and biting all over his neck. *Not Ben. Not Ben. Not Ben.*

His voice was uneven with my heavy thrusts as he gasped, "Just... say... it..."

No. I groaned, and it almost slipped before I caught myself. Our bodies were slick with sweat as we fucked so raw I was coming undone.

"I want you to..." he whispered through a hoarse breath, fingers digging into the sheets. "I want to be him for you."

Fuck me. No... This is so wrong...

God, Ben... please. I love you, baby. Please... love me.

"Fucking... *fuck*..." I grunted, my hips slamming into his, causing him to cry out.

He was going to come soon, I could feel it. He tried reaching for his dick, but I wouldn't let him. Keeping him trapped between my weight and the mattress, I was determined to get him off with no hands.

"Tell me..." Tate commanded, voice jagged and about to snap.

Fuck...

"Fuck... I'm sorry..." I roared, resting my forehead on his back as I squeezed my eyes shut tight.

And I imagined.

"Ben..." I mewled softly as my dick pulsed. "I love you, baby. Oh God, *Ben*..."

Tate hummed with his face in the pillow.

Baby... I love you so much. I love fucking you, Ben...

"Jesus, you feel so good, baby..." I began falling, succumbing to the sensations. "I'm coming... Fuck, I'm coming in you... Ben!"

I sobbed breathlessly as the climax ripped through my loins, my dick throbbing hard inside his ass. My whole body was tingling from head to toe. And I was still speaking...

"I love you, Ben. I love you so fucking much. I'm sorry..."

Tate's voice was deep and echoey as he let go, finding his own release. My hips slowed and my tortured voice finally went quiet.

And we were left panting in the dark.

Empty.

After the five-hour drive, I made it home in one piece.

It was Christmas Day, and I hadn't planned on being back yet. I knew Alec and Kayla were likely inside with her parents, opening presents together as a family.

And I was there to crash their fun. The lonely loser with no one, who left the home of his random fuck-buddy because his other fuck-buddies couldn't have him around.

Tate and I had woken up that morning as if nothing happened. We ignored the awkwardness of me fucking him while pretending he was Ben, and just ate breakfast together, chit-chatting about nothing.

And then I left.

I didn't tell him I would call him, because he knew I wouldn't. What he didn't know was that it wasn't because I didn't like him, or because I never wanted to see him again. It was because I wouldn't be around, so calling him would make no sense.

I drove slow the whole way back to ABQ, knowing that showing up at the apartment on Christmas would open me up to all kinds of prodding from my friends. But that didn't much matter either, because I was on a bit of a deadline at the moment.

I needed to start packing.

I finally mustered the strength to get out of my car and ambled inside. Sure enough, there were Alec and Kayla, and her parents, sitting around in the living room sipping hot cocoa.

Swallowing down the uncomfortable burning tension inside me and ignoring the feeling of unwelcomeness flooding my body, I grunted *hey* and staggered toward my room. I almost made it, too...

"Ryan?" Alec's voice beckoned from behind me, causing me to stop in place. "What are you doing back so soon?"

He and Kayla were immediately at my side, as were Kayla's parents, who were clearly expecting the whole introduction thing. I barely managed to shake their hands and tell them my name before turning and jaunting quickly, and awkwardly, into my room.

"Hey..." Kayla chirped as they followed me. "Is everything okay?"

The dam was about to burst. I couldn't face them. I knew I was just going to spill it; all the drama from the past week since I left, lying and telling them I was going to Denver to be with my mom, when in reality I had gone straight to Ben and Jess's like a desperate little puppy.

"Ryan... what's up, man?" Alec asked with worry lining his tone.

Kayla placed her hand on my shoulder and I squeezed my eyes shut. Dropping my bag, I sighed, my shoulders sagging in defeat as I turned to my friends. My anguish was clearly written all over my face because they both instantly pouted and wrapped me up in a ridiculous group hug that would've felt much more patronizing if I weren't on the verge of an emotional breakdown.

"Come on..." Alec crooned, bringing me over to my bed and sitting me down, plopping next to me. "Tell us what happened."

Kayla disappeared for a moment to let her parents know we needed to have a pow-wow real quick, and I started spilling my guts to my best friend, releasing my demons, and the whole story about Ben and Jess, the blinding happiness of being with them for days, then the break-up, Tate, the party, the fight, and landing on the last and most crucial part of it all... My departure.

"So... You're really leaving?" Alec mumbled, clearly trying to sound a little more macho and unaffected, but his eyes were giving him away. I felt like a real asshole for making him look like that.

I nodded slowly. "I think... I just need a fresh start, ya know? After everything with Ben and Jess and Hailey... I just gotta go. I can't be here anymore."

"And you've already been accepted?" Kayla asked, rubbing my back in methodical circles, which was actually calming me down a lot. She was such a great person. *My best friend is a lucky guy.*

I just want to have that some day... And I need to get away from here. Away from the memories of the people I want it with...

"Yea," I sighed out hard. "My flight is in two days."

"Where will you stay?" Alec asked. "Dorms?"

I shook my head. "My aunt lives out there. I already called her from the car. She said she's happy to let me stay with her. Actually, she sounded pretty excited. She lives alone and all..."

The two of them nodded, but the mood in the room was grim. Alec and I had been best friends since freshman orientation. We had just clicked right away, so much so that we decided to rent this place together, and living together ever since. It would be a big adjustment, not having him around.

"I'm... *fuck*," Alec grunted, shaking his head, eyes stuck on the floor. "I'm gonna miss you, Ryan. You've been like a brother to me."

I saw him squeeze Kayla's hand and I was choking back tears. It sucked. The whole thing just sucked so bad. I didn't really *want* to leave. But I *had* to.

I needed to go somewhere else and experience life. I

needed to be free, far away from these painful memories and the people they were centered around.

"You'll always be my brother, Alec," I told him, turning to face them both. "I could move to the fucking moon and you wouldn't get rid of me. I promise."

He smiled and Kayla giggled out a tiny sob, which brought my attention to the fact that she was crying.

"And you, Kale..." I started, taking her chin in my fingers. "Take care of him, please. And don't take any of his shit." She laughed softly, half-crying, hugging onto Alec's side. "Promise?"

She giggled through a breath and nodded. "I promise."

Sighing, I nodded to myself. "Good. Okay, well... I need to pack. So get back to your parents and enjoy your Christmas."

The two of them obliged, though there was an obvious damper on the day, thanks to yours truly. I was really trying to stow the guilt from my many fuck-ups over the past month, and just focus on what I needed to do. *I suppose I could let myself stew in my misery once I'm on the plane...*

Hours later, I was almost done packing. Understandably, I wasn't taking everything I owned to my aunt's; just the essentials. Alec claimed he was going to keep my bedroom for me in case I came back, or use it as a guest room, but I urged him to sell my stuff and find a new roommate. I had to be firm and a bit distant, otherwise I would cave and talk myself out of the whole thing.

I just kept remembering Hailey's advice from last night...

I needed to find my path. I couldn't just stay there and torture myself. I was young. I had my whole life ahead of me, and it was time I started making an effort to find out who *I* was. I needed to stop letting others control my happiness.

I was stuffing my laptop into my overnight bag when my

fingers brushed something hard, yet soft to the touch. I knew what it was right away, and tugged it out of my bag.

My heart pounded against my ribcage as I stared at the journal in my hands. The rose beneath the clear plastic; the three falling petals.

My throat constricted and suddenly I couldn't breathe.

The tears I had been holding back since last night finally forced their way out.

I hugged the last remaining piece of them close to my chest, begging, *praying* for some relief from this broken heart, even though I knew it wouldn't come.

I'd been through break-ups before. I knew that as much as it hurt, *time* was ultimately the only thing which would heal my wounds. That, and some distance.

BOSTON WAS BEAUTIFUL. Beautiful and fucking freezing.

It had been about a week since I said goodbye to my best friends, and my life in New Mexico. Two days after Christmas, I boarded a plane to Logan Airport and didn't look back. I couldn't, because if I was being honest with myself, I had left half of my heart back in the Southwest, and I wasn't entirely sure I'd be able to survive without it.

I was trudging through the snow, making my way home after spending almost two hours in the law library of Suffolk University, locating all the books I would need to start classes tomorrow. Transferring mid-semester wasn't something that people typically opted for, mainly because it was a huge pain in the ass for everyone involved. But the school would let you do it if you plead your case well enough. And paid the semester's tuition in full, up front.

Say goodbye to all your money, genius. This little escape plan of yours just left you with a whopping eighty-five dollars in your bank account.

I tried to stop mentally scolding myself and remember that Jill, my aunt, had offered to lend me some money if I needed it. Not that I would take it unless I was truly in dire straits. She was already letting me live with her for free, and had bought me an unlimited Charlie Card so I could get to and from school on the green line.

I didn't need money for anything anyway. I was a struggling student, putting himself through law school. It was expected that I'd be flat broke. I could get a job bartending or something, if it came to that. But as it stood, I just didn't have time for anything other than school. Jill was feeding me and putting a roof over my head. I didn't need much else for the time being.

I took the steps down into the train station slowly because everything was covered in ice, and I had already almost busted my ass four times since I left the house that morning. Jill thought it was hilarious how out of my element I was in New England. I hadn't been around snow in years and clearly I'd forgotten how to act.

The train was approaching as I was scanning my card, so I had to hustle to catch it before it left, slipping for the fifth time, but managing not to fall and embarrass myself. Crashing into a nearby seat, I yanked my heavy backpack, overflowing with books, off my shoulder, dropping it into my lap.

My nerves were getting to me. The idea of starting school tomorrow was stressing me out, and I felt insecurities creeping through my mind that I hadn't felt since I started UNM. Meeting new people, making new friends, dealing with new professors... Especially halfway through the semester. It wasn't going to be easy.

Fortunately for me, all this new drama was serving its purpose. Distracting me from the hole in my heart, which was still so sore it felt like an open wound.

I thought about Ben and Jessica constantly. I just couldn't get them off my mind, ever, and I hadn't heard a word from either of them since New Year's Eve.

I had been hanging out with my aunt. Some might say that spending New Year's Eve with a gaggle of middle-aged ladies, smoking cigarettes and drinking Pabst, would't be an ideal way to count down to a new year. But I was nursing some serious heart-ache, so for me it worked out just fine. Plus, Jill's friends loved me. I was young and hot, in their eyes, so they spent most of the evening teasing me and making shameless comments about my abs, until my aunt had to threaten them with physical violence.

We were drinking and playing Keno at a local bar in Allston when Jess called me. And of course I didn't answer. I couldn't. There was no way I could hear her voice... It would destroy me.

So I let the phone ring, all the while gaping at it like it contained the mark of the beast, until the call ended. And that was it. Not another peep, from either of them.

Of course, I *had* blocked Ben's number right after leaving his house on Christmas Eve, because I knew I needed to. If I was going to be strong and move on with my life, I couldn't risk him trying to get to me, not even by message. Which was why I had also deleted my Instagram account.

Actively halting my mind from doing what it was doing, I opened my bag, taking out the one piece of them I allowed myself to hang onto...

The journal.

I flipped through the pages, skimming over some of my poems and songs I'd written in the past few days. It was an outlet I never thought I'd turn to, but surprisingly it was helping me get out some of the emotions which were always begging to be set free. I knew I'd never show them to anyone. This journal was my own safe space, dedicated to capturing the words I wouldn't allow myself to speak, or even think. Getting it out on paper helped. It pacified me, if even just for a few moments.

The journal was still practically new, most of it still empty, but I just loved the feel of the paper. It was soft and smooth under my fingers, and as I flicked the pages quickly with my thumb, brushing to the very end, something caught my eye.

There was writing on the second-to-last page.

My pulse immediately sped up as I hesitantly opened the journal to the page with the writing.

Dear Ryan,

I blinked hard, my lip quivering.

It was a letter. And I knew right away, without reading anything else, that it wasn't from Jess.

It was a letter from Ben.

My hands began to tremble as my chest tightened, making it hard to breathe. I squeezed my eyes closed and slapped the journal shut fast. I couldn't read that. No way. It would completely derail everything.

Whatever he had to say, I couldn't possibly hear, or read, right now. I wasn't strong enough.

But everything inside me was vibrating with a curiosity fueled by longing that was so strong it actually forced my hands to open the journal back up.

I peeked at the page, biting down on my lower lip as I began to read...

My eyes savored every single word he had written, absorbing them and letting them seep into my brain. By the time I reached his signature at the end, I had read the letter a hundred times and missed my stop, riding the train all the way to the end, where it turned around and came back. And I was still reading.

Still quaking down to my core.

Still hungry for more words... more declarations. More Ben.

He said he loved me.

No. Loves. Present tense.

He. Loves. Me.

My eyes were so wide I could feel them drying out. I couldn't blink. Fuck, I could barely move.

I just kept reading that word, over and over and over again until I felt like every nerve in my body was being snipped at the end.

I love you.

I'll never stop loving you.

Give me the chance.

He wants a chance.

He loves me.

Ben Lockwood loves me.

I felt crippled. Distraught. Wrecked down to my soul.

There was no way for me to react, other than to just keep reading it, and imagine him saying it, out loud, to me.

My grief turned into hope, then quickly morphed into regret, followed lastly by anger.

Why couldn't Ben have just said these things when we were together? Why did it take me walking out on him to realize what I had known in my heart since day one?

Why was he so selfish and stupid and fucking *evil*??

My brain was throbbing inside my skull, and I felt a migraine like no other coming on. Thankfully that time I was able to detach my eyes from the journal long enough to notice my stop, and get off the damn train.

Stomping through the leftover snow from the storm that had happened the day after I arrived, I made my way inside my aunt's apartment. Luckily for me, she was out, so I wouldn't have to explain my next few moves to her. Because they weren't the actions of a sane, rational human being.

The second I set foot inside the apartment, I grabbed the first thing I saw, an umbrella, and used it to smash everything in sight. Nothing that my aunt cared for, obviously. Nothing irreplaceable. Just the walls, the door, the table, the floor... basically everything in the immediate vicinity.

I whacked and thumped that stupid umbrella against everything I could reach, heaving and panting, growling and snarling in a complete fury of nonsense. Because I wanted to hurt something, but I couldn't. *I* was the one hurting. It was incredibly frustrating.

Once I was done with my temper tantrum, and the umbrella was broken in half looking equally pathetic, huffed my way over to the kitchen, opened the fridge and freezer at the same time, removing a six-pack of Pabst and a container of ice cream. I sat on the floor, shotgunned two beers, then ate the entire half-gallon of rocky road like some kind of ridiculous loser.

I couldn't remember ever feeling so completely fucked.

The rest of the afternoon went by in a blur.

I killed the rest of the beers, then sat in the shower, hugging my knees to my chest for about an hour. After that, so damn fed up with myself, I decided to do something more productive.

Like get laid.

I wasn't proud of my juvenile decision, but honestly it was the only way I felt like I could cope with the fact that the man I wanted more than anyone or anything in the world, the same one who told me that I *couldn't* love him, now loved me. Now that I was across the country, *moving on.*

I didn't want to think about Ben anymore. I didn't want to think about Jess anymore. I just wanted to forget that they existed for like a millisecond.

So I took the train back into the city, found a bar that was in that perfect sweet spot between dive and bougie, took a seat and just waited.

That was my plan. Whoever approached me first, if I was attracted to them, then it was on. I didn't even give a fuck; girl, guy, whatever. I just needed a hot body to take away all these feelings. They were way too much for me to bear.

And sure enough, ten minutes into my excursion, I was approached by a gorgeous blonde with big, obviously fake tits. *So I guess this is happening...*

The girl's pick-up line was that she lived right around the corner, which I actually appreciated, although I didn't want to make it a whole *thing...* I would have preferred a random bathroom hook-up, but she looked a little too classy for that.

She was clearly older than me, probably around Jess's age, though she looked older than Jessica, which didn't say much. Jess looked like she was still in her twenties anyway.

Wow, really? You're going to think about them this whole time?? What's the fucking point then?

Forcing my mind to switch off as I played the game with the woman, I flirted and bought her a drink, both of us killing them fast so that we could bounce. She brought me around the corner to her insanely nice apartment in the downtown high-rise, all the while telling me about her divorce like I really gave a fuck.

I knew I was coming off like a chauvinistic dick-wad, but I

couldn't help myself. I just needed it to be purely physical. A distraction from the chaos going on inside me.

Once securely inside her million-dollar apartment, likely a parting gift from her wealthy ex-husband, she came at me like an animal. Kissing me all over, touching my chest and my stomach, my ass. She was clearly horny as fuck, and I was unprepared.

No fucking clue what I'm doing.

"What's your name?" She asked while tonguing my earlobe, holding my hand on one of her overly firm tits.

"Ryan," I grunted, plopping down on the nearest piece of furniture, a couch, and bringing her with me. "Yours?"

"Kelly," she purred, sliding down the straps of her dress to let the breasts free. They were giant. I had never seen fake boobs, or really *any* boobs, so big before in my life.

Kelly climbed on top of me, straddling my waist and pushing me down horizontal as she licked and kissed all over my neck and throat, yanking my shirt up over my head. Her lips trailed down my chest, tongue gliding through every sinew of the muscles in my torso until she reached my pants. They were undone and tugged down in record time, and then my semi-hard cock was in her mouth so fast it was like she was trying to win a race of some kind.

God, what is going on?? This is all happening so fast... I don't even really want to do this. Why am I doing this again?

Oh right, Ben loves me.

Fuck.

Her tongue swirled around the head of my cock before she sucked the rest of me between her parted lips, deep-throating like she fucking invented it. It felt good, in an obvious kind of way, but my dick was hardening more at the memory of Ben's letter...

He loves me.

He wrote that before the party on Christmas Eve. So that means... he punched Tate because he's in love with me. And he was jealous.

For some reason, the idea of Ben being jealous sent a surge of rushing blood directly into my cock. I was suddenly so hard I could feel my erection throbbing in the chick's mouth.

She tugged her lips off, stroking me hard in her hand. "You have such an awesome dick."

I shrugged to myself, leaning my head back. "Thanks..."

Ben loves me. And Jess loves me, too.

They're probably sad without me. They're probably missing me right now...

My mind began to wander while Kelly the cock-fiend sucked me again, harder.

Maybe they're fucking right now... Maybe they're thinking about me while they fuck.

I remembered the first time I saw them, on Thanksgiving night... When I watched them together.

A groan slipped.

Kelly took the noise to mean that I was ready to slide my cock inside her pussy, and sat up fast, shimmying out of her form-fitting dress. She was in only her panties, and she looked really good. But I had to acknowledge the work she had done, and how much I preferred my women natural.

One woman, in particular...

Oh my God, shut up, brain!

She slithered out of her panties and climbed over me. "Do you have a condom?"

I froze, gaping up at her in uncertainty. "Kelly, I can't fuck you." I shook my head in a solemn sort of way, as if I were delivering terrible news.

"Why not?" She scoffed, running her hands up my chest.

"Because, I'm going through a break-up, and I'm... still in

love with..." my voice trailed off. I refrained from finishing my sentence, because it would just open up the floor to questions I had no intention of answering.

Kelly stared at me for a moment, seemingly in thought. "You poor thing." She pouted, tracing my abs with her index finger. "My divorce was pretty clean and easy. I mean, on my end. My ex is an investment banker in his late fifties, so... you know..."

She gave me a look, and I nodded in understanding of what she was saying. She married for the money, and she got it.

"Do you want to talk about it?" She smirked down at me, and I grinned.

"Absolutely not," I rumbled, pulling her down to me. "I'm not going to fuck you..." She whimpered. "But I *will* make you come."

She giggled and I kissed her neck, while she rubbed her naked tits on my chest. It felt so odd. They were insanely firm. But her nipples were peaked, and that I enjoyed. I took one between my lips and sucked hard, making her moan.

I flipped her beneath me and worked over her nipples with my mouth, while my hand slinked between her thighs. I swirled my fingers around in her wetness, listening to her uneven breaths as I sunk two inside her slowly.

"Uh God!" She gasped with a fistful of my hair while I thrusted my fingers in and out of her hard, curling them a bit to graze her g-spot.

Keeping my eyes closed, I ground my hips against her thigh, begging for some friction relief. Kelly fisted my cock in her hand and jerked me off while I fingered her, like we were fucking teenagers.

But it was enough to keep my mind from drifting where it didn't belong.

Don't get me wrong, I was still thinking about Ben and

Jess. But this time I was using them as motivation for what I was doing. In my mind, I imagined Ben and Jessica watching me, with this random lady, acting like a sexy moron. I liked it.

I liked thinking about them being jealous, and thinking about me. Wanting me. *Missing* me.

At some point I was sure they'd move on. They would stop missing me and go back to their lives, as if *we* had never happened. But for right now, I had to believe they were feeling what I was.

I made Kelly come on my fingers, then she sucked me to orgasm between her soft lips.

And then I left. As simple as that.

I took an Uber back to my aunt's apartment, took a shower, and got ready for my first day of classes.

And when I lied down in bed with a hard sigh, I wondered when this emptiness would cease. Picking up my journal, I flipped to the second-to-last page, gazing over the handwriting with my tired eyes.

My fingers brushed the paper, the words; feeling them.

Ben loved me. He loved me, but it was too late.

Wasn't it?

BEN
Two Weeks After Thailand

"I should leave..." Ryan whispered, his voice all but trembling. It was so cute, I just wanted to kiss him all over his adorable, worried face.

"Baby, don't be ridiculous," Jess murmured, pecking him on the cheek as she passed by holding a tray of fancy cheeses, meats, and other assorted gourmet goodies. *Charcuterie*, she called it, I think.

Whatever. Just a bunch of stuff to distract our friends from the inevitable freak-out.

On the outside, tonight seemed like just a regular Thursday night dinner at our house with our best friends. But in actuality, this night was likely to be one that none of us would soon forget.

Because we had invited them all over to finally tell the truth.

We'd been dodging our friends for all too long. We hadn't even seen them since before I left for Boston, and we'd been avoiding their calls since we got back from Thailand, so it was definitely time. We couldn't leave them in the dark any longer.

So Jess, Ryan and I were hosting this dinner party together to come clean about how we'd gone from a regular old married couple to a polyamorous throuple involving our daughter's ex-boyfriend.

Pretty much everyone else in our lives knew at that point. We had just told Hailey last weekend. And all things considered, she took it pretty damn well.

Naturally she was confused. She was hurt that we had been lying to her, and she was baffled at how our bizarre relationship with her ex even came to be. She could obviously understand how something like that might happen with maybe one parent... But with both of us?

It was beyond strange. Honestly, the whole thing was straight out of the movies. Sometimes I could still barely believe it myself.

We left Hailey last weekend feeling content after finally admitting the truth of the situation. Fortunately she didn't want many details, so me throwing myself off a bridge out of awkwardness wasn't necessary. She seemed placated by the simple fact that we were happy; that our love was so overpowering, we wouldn't have been able to give it up, which was why we brought Ryan back from Boston and moved him into our home.

She was accepting of all that due to one main factor: Hailey believed in true love conquering all.

My daughter was a romantic. She loved reading those books... The ones with the shirtless guys on the covers. I used to think they were smut, but she'd argued with me over the years that they were all love stories, and that she loved the fairy tale aspect of it, even in the ones that weren't about knights and princesses. She told me that even the dark love stories had happy endings, and it made her heart full.

She could tell from Jess and I confessing the truth about our relationship with Ryan that we had found *our* happy ending. It just happened to be one very different than your standard romance. But I admired our story. Hell, I was *proud* of it. We were different.

Our relationship was as real as one could get. We were married, after all. But barring that fact, the three of us didn't like to label ourselves. Ryan had started referring to himself as bisexual, because he was attracted to both men and women, although he still swore he had never even looked at another guy before me. I sort of like that...

I, on the other hand, chose to call myself *pansexual*, if I had to pick a word. Because I still hadn't really found myself attracted to men who weren't Ryan. He was the only guy I looked at. And while I'd definitely checked out women other than Jess, I certainly wasn't attracted to another man in that way. And pansexuality was the attraction to anyone, based solely on your feelings for that person, and his, her, or their soul; the gender having nothing to do with it. I liked that concept. *Love is love, no matter what it looks like.*

I wasn't sure if I'd ever be attracted to a man other than Ryan-never say never right? But for the foreseeable future, he was it. He and Jessica were my everythings. My lovers, my friends, my confidantes, my partners in crime. *My husband and wife.* The two people who made my heart beat faster and my insides tingle with every notion of excitement I could relish. They were my world.

Them, and my kids.

Speaking of kids, this was the other reason why telling our friends the truth now was so important. Jessica was due in less than two months. Everyone would want to be around to see the baby once he graced us with his presence, and Ryan was here. He lived *here*, and was preparing for a baby, alongside his spouses.

As much as our friends deserved to know what was going on, Ryan deserved recognition as our partner. We'd already spent too much time hiding him, and downplaying his feelings as *the fling*. It was fucked up. We wanted to show him off. After all, he was sharing his life with us. It was about time we started sharing ours with him, too.

Our friends are going to completely lose their minds. It's just a fact.

Wrapping my arm around Ryan's waist, I pulled him flush against me. His eyes were wide, his forehead lined from the unease. I couldn't resist. I kissed the small *v* between his brows.

"You're not allowed to leave, husband," I crooned, moving my kissing to the hallow of his neck as his rapid pulse thrummed on my lips. "You already said, 'I do'. There's no turning back now."

"No, I know that," he huffed then swallowed hard as he leaned into me for support. I loved when he did that.

Ryan was so damned independent; used to handling everything on his own. But ever since I brought him back from Boston to be with us, he'd begun letting us in more. I knew he didn't want to burden people with his issues, but we'd vowed to ease him of such hardships, and we meant to do just that. I could tell he was finally starting to accept it.

"I just mean like, we don't have to do this now," he gulped, tugging my face back to stop my sensual kisses.

Maybe I was getting carried away, but I couldn't help myself. I'd gone six long months without him. The honeymoon in Thailand was all well and good, but I still needed my man. Constantly.

It was starting to become dangerous.

"I can go assemble the Pack n' Play in the shed while you guys do your dinner thing," Ryan muttered, gliding his thumb over my bottom lip.

"Are you high?" I bit the tip of his thumb playfully. "The

only reason we're doing this is to tell them about you. Otherwise I'd sooner be downstairs, Netflix and chilling." He chuckled, and I grinned. "Or in the shower..."

He laughed again and shook his head while I wiggled my brows at him.

"I'm just so nervous," he sighed and began yanking me by the hand over to the liquor cabinet. "What are you going to say to them? What if they freak out? What if they scream or cry, or make a huge deal on social media??" He poured us each a glass of scotch, clinking his on mine quick before taking a slow sip.

"Ryan, if *Hailey* didn't do any of those things, what makes you think Jess's sister or my stupid friends will?" I raised a commanding brow at him, to which he shrugged and sipped his drink again. "Honestly, she was the only person who had the right to act crazy over this. And she was fine. I mean, not exactly *fine*... But she was able to be happy for us."

"Yea, she *said* that," he grumbled, killing his drink already and going in for another. "But it'll be a totally different story when she actually *sees* us together with her own two eyes."

"Well, we'll just have to *try* not to hang all over each other," I grinned, and he stifled a laugh. "I know it'll be like torture for you to keep your hands off, but I'm sure if you try real hard, you can swing it. I believe in you." I winked at him and he growled, narrowing his eyes. *I love that look.*

"Ryan!" Jess yelped, and he was instantly darting out of the room to help her.

Sighing, I followed his lead, checking to see if I could be of some assistance, although usually the two of them took over in the kitchen, and I was lucky if I got to sneak a quick taste of whatever they were doing before they kicked me out. I truly enjoyed our dynamic, though. More than I ever could have anticipated. Everything we did just seemed to work.

I turned the corner, sipping from my glass and watching as

Ryan pulled a pan of brownies out of the oven. *The smell in this place... My mouth is watering.*

"Babe, aren't you going a little overboard here?" I asked my wife, lifting a brow in her direction.

"No," she hummed with finality. *Well, alright then.* "I just want to make sure there's a wide selection of treats to distract them from all of the probing questions they'll be wanting to ask."

"Hmm... actually that's a good point." I strolled over to place a kiss on top of her head. "This all looks amazing, baby."

She smiled with pride. "Thanks. It's weird, I think the baby likes when I cook. Maybe he or she will be a chef someday!" She gasped, her eyes widening and sparkling in excitement.

I chuckled softly, running my hand over her round belly. "Maybe."

Ryan and I helped Jess get everything set up in the dining room. Our guests were due to arrive any minute, and I was starting to agree with Jess's plan. Distracting them with food and drinks seemed like a solid way to go.

The doorbell rang as I was pouring myself a second drink, and warning Ryan to slow down with my eyes while he poured himself a third.

Jess beat us to the door, answering it with her usual enthusiasm, which our friends seemed to accept. And in walked Jess's sister, Marie, and her husband Greg, along with our best friends since middle school, Bill and Rachel. *Hm, they all arrived together. Was that planned?*

"Come on in, guys!" Jess squealed, but I was distracted from her anxious tone by Ryan squeezing my hand so damn hard I felt bones crunching. He tossed back his drink and gave me a panicked look.

"Baby, relax," I whispered to him, rubbing his back slowly. "Breathe for me." He took a deep pull and held it in for a moment, then let it go slowly. "Good. Everything's gonna be fine, alright, gorgeous? We're doing this together, and nothing they could say or do will change anything about us, so really it doesn't fucking matter at all."

"I love you, Ben," he whimpered by my ear, his voice quivering. *Holy shit, he's really nervous. Fuck, I need to help him out. Make this a little easier on the poor kid.*

"I love you too, baby," I told him with assurance. "Everything is golden. Right?"

I gave him a megawatt smile, and he finally let a timid grin slip, glancing at the floor as he nodded.

"See? There's that beautiful smile," I rasped, tapping his chin with my knuckles. He smacked me on the ass and I laughed. *My man's back.*

"I found an amazing recipe for buffalo chicken dip on Pinterest, so there's that... And a meat, cheese, and fruit plate. Mini quiches... Those were frozen though..." Jess was rambling as she guided our friends into the house.

As soon as they were out of the foyer and making their way to the dining room, we saw them. And they saw us.

Everyone froze. All eyes on me and Ryan.

The silence stretched through the entire house, like a giant balloon, filling up the whole place.

A throat cleared.

It was mine. "Hey, guys!" I threw on my biggest, fakest charm-you-out-of-your-panties smile, cocking my head to the side. "How's everyone doing?"

No one responded. They all just stared at me, then Ryan, then each other.

I felt like I should nudge Ryan to get him speaking, but he seemed somewhat stiff himself. So I took matters into my own hands.

"You all remember Ryan, right?" I gestured to Ryan, as if they could have possibly forgotten who he was.

Sure. They'd probably forget who the president was before they could forget about Ryan Harper after that little show on Christmas Eve.

The quiet continued for few more excruciating seconds, before Jess's best friend chimed in.

"Of course," Rachel murmured, giving Ryan a polite, if not obviously confused, smile. "Hi, Ryan! Good to see you again."

My husband finally pulled himself together, swallowing visibly before his lips curved and he showed off those sexy dimples.

"Yea, you all too," he hummed, shaking Greg and Bill's hands, then going for kisses on the cheeks of the ladies.

"So what are you doing here?" Greg was the first one to ask, and Marie shot him a look. "Is Hailey home?" He started looking around.

"Or Tate?" Bill sneered, and the two of them started chuckling.

Dear Lord.

My patience for this whole stupid charade wore thin in an instant. *I'm done with this.*

"Nope. He's here with us," I spoke firm yet casual, then grabbed Ryan's hand. "You guys want some food? That damn charcuterie looks delicious."

I dragged Ryan into the dining room, Jess following closely behind us. Ryan pulled out a chair for her and helped her sit down. Everyone was *staring* at us.

"So Ryan, did you come all the way from Albuquerque just for the buffalo chicken dip?" Bill asked with humor in his voice, though his eyes were serious, and aimed directly at me. He knew something was up.

"Uhh... no. No, can't say that I did." Ryan peeked at me.

I knew the look. It meant he wanted me to save him, but honestly there wasn't much I could do. We were already sliding on ice. It was time to steer into the skid.

"You guys are probably wondering why we haven't seen you in a while..." I started, cautiously. "Or, ya know... returned your calls."

"Um, yea," Greg huffed, sidling over to the food.

"We heard you went to Thailand..." Jess's sister added, cocking her head as she watched Ryan huddled up at Jess's side.

"We did," I nodded, and said nothing more. It was excruciatingly awkward, standing around trying to figure out how to say what we needed to say, when all of their minds were likely running crazy with assumptions.

"What's in Thailand?" Greg asked while shoving cheese into his mouth.

"We stayed at a gorgeous resort," Jess jumped in, glancing up at Ryan with a smile. "Private, right on the water. It was tropical and just so damn beautiful. I want to go back."

She tugged his hand, and he grinned. "Me too."

Memories of the two of them in the pool flooded my mind, almost transporting me back there. It was truly one of the best times of my entire life. *If I could be back there right now with them, I so would. In a heartbeat.*

"You were there?!" Greg coughed, choking on whatever he was chewing. Everyone's eyes set on Ryan, and his mouth dropped open, no words coming out.

I sighed out loud. "Yes, he was there. Guys, let's just address the goddamned elephant in the room so we can get this over with and move on. Ryan lives here."

And then I stopped talking.

I probably should have kept going and elaborated a bit more, but honestly the looks on their faces were pretty hilarious, and I enjoyed seeing them completely shocked like that.

"What do you mean he... *lives* here?" Bill asked, quietly.

"Like, you're letting him stay here...?" Rachel added, clearly trying to make some sense of it in her mind.

I shook my head slowly. "No. I mean he lives here *with* us."

"*With* you?" Greg huffed. "Like a... roommate?"

"No, not that either," I answered. "We're... together."

"What is really going on right now?" Marie asked, focusing on her sister, who was doing nothing more than methodically rubbing her belly and staring at me.

I shrugged at Jess and Ryan, and they shrugged back.

"The three of us..." I gulped, struggling to figure out how to phrase it in the most uncomplicated way. There weren't many options... It was super complicated. "We got married in Thailand. So... ya know... Ryan lives with us, and he's going to be a father to our baby... *with* us. The three of us."

I let out a hard breath, feeling like I might fall over. It was one of the more strenuous things I'd ever had to get out in my entire life. Not that I was unsure of anything. I loved my husband more than any words could describe, but telling our friends, the people we'd known for almost our entire lives, was a challenge.

Because this was always when the questions started.

"What the hell are you talking about??"

"How would you get married? You're already married!"

"That's not legal, is it?"

"You mean, he slept with your wife?"

"How did this all happen?"

"Does Hailey know?"

"What's in this dip? It really is delicious."

"Guys, oh my God, can you please shut up for a second?!" I

barked, raking my hand through my hair. "You're making me want to blow my brains out."

"Well, you can't just drop a bomb on us like this and expect us not to have questions!" Bill retorted, and Rachel shushed him.

"Honey, just relax," she whispered to her husband. "Let's not freak out or anything. These are our best friends in the world. I'm sure they know what they're doing... Right?"

She glanced at Jess, giving her a pleading look.

Jess was quiet for a moment, chewing on her lower lip. Then she finally spoke up. "Everything Ben said is right. We've been seeing Ryan for a while... After the drama on Christmas Eve, he left and moved to Boston to get away. But then I found out I was pregnant, and we knew we didn't want to be without him. So Ben went and got him, brought him home, and well... here we are." She shrugged.

"You're making this sound incredibly casual, Jessie," Marie breathed, shaking her head. "This is Hailey's ex boyfriend we're talking about. And now you're saying he might be the father of your baby?! That's insane!"

"No. Not *might be*," I growled, trying hard to rein in my temper. "He *is* the father of our baby. And so am I."

"This is the weirdest shit I've ever heard," Greg chuckled to himself as he continued eating.

"Yea, we know it's weird," Jess sighed. "We're not trying to make it normal. We don't care about being normal! We're just in love. That's it. And if you guys can't accept that, then we have nothing else to talk about."

She looked like she wanted to stand up and storm off in a huff, but her stomach was too big and heavy. So she crossed her arms over her chest and pouted. I laughed softly, then leaned up against the table next to her and Ryan.

"So... Hailey does know?" Bill finally broke the silence and the sounds of Greg munching.

"Yup," I nodded.

"And... she's okay with it?" Marie asked, appearing skeptical.

"It was a little rocky at first, but you know Hailey," I told them. "She's got a great head on her shoulders, and she just wants us to be happy. Look, we just wanted to be up-front with you, because you're our best friends. We're still *us*... Just happier."

"And now there's three of us instead of two," Jess added with a smile. Ryan kissed her head.

"You've been awfully quiet throughout this confession, kid," Bill said to Ryan, raising his brow. "Blink twice if you're being held against your will."

I laughed out loud, and Ryan chuckled along, shaking his head.

"I don't really know what to say..." he murmured, slinking his arm around my waist. "I didn't plan on this happening. None of us did. But I guess... the heart wants what the heart wants."

"Hm, cliche," Rachel giggled.

"It's true," he shrugged, smothering his smile as he glanced at me. I winked at his beautiful face.

"So you're a *throuple*?" Greg sighed. "This is going to completely throw off the teams for game night, you know that right?"

The three of us laughed, and I announced, "I'll gladly sit some out."

"Uh, I'm fine with that!" Marie squealed. "He's like shockingly good at Scategories and I'm over it."

Ryan nudged my side. "You're good at Scategories?"

"There are still so many things you don't know about me, kid," I grinned and he bit his lip.

"Okay, well let's sit down and have some of this food before Greg eats it all," Bill pulled out a chair. "I have tons more questions."

I rolled my eyes and Ryan laughed softly, plopping down next to Jessica, squeezing her hand tight with his. I could sense the relief radiating off of him, and it made me beyond happy. He was finally here. Fully part of our lives, etched into our world.

He wasn't going anywhere.

HOURS LATER, the food had been enjoyed, and the drinks had definitely been flowing.

The girls were in the kitchen sipping wine, with Ryan, who was showing them all pictures from our wedding in Thailand. I had to take him at his word that he'd saved the dirty ones in a private folder.

Greg, Bill, and me were downstairs in the man cave, drinking scotch, smoking cigars, and watching baseball on the huge TV.

"So I have another question," Bill picked back up again, and I was seriously about to punch him.

"Oh my God, you have to stop," I groaned, squeezing my eyes shut and pinching the bridge of my nose with my fingers. *He's giving me the worst headache ever.*

"No, I mean it. This one's important," he turned to face me, sloshing his drink around in his glass.

"Don't spill that on my couch, and what the fuck is it now?" I grumbled.

"So you like... hook up with Ryan...?" His voice came out quiet and hesitant, like he wasn't supposed to be asking me that, which was slightly accurate, since it wasn't any of his business. But we'd been friends since we were kids. Obviously we talked about sex. "Like, you guys... *do it*?"

"No, we don't," I muttered sarcastically. "It's fully platonic." I rolled my eyes at him. "Of course we do! He's my fucking husband."

"That's nuts," Greg snickered, giving away his state of inebriation.

"I'm sorry! I just never knew you were..." Bill's voice trailed off.

"What? Gay?" I narrowed my gaze at him. He shrugged, to which I scoffed and shook my head.

"Have you ever hooked up with Tate?" He asked again, still quiet, as if he expected Tate to be right around the corner.

"Uh, no." I mimicked gagging. "Why would you ask me that? Because Tate is the only gay guy you know, so obviously now that I like dick I must have hooked up with him?"

"I know other gay guys..." he mumbled with petulance. *Yea, right.*

"Bill, I'm not gay." I sipped my drink slowly. "I'm not attracted to miscellaneous dudes."

"Only Ryan?"

"Yea..."

"Why?"

"I don't know. Because I love him." I gave him a pointed look. I had never seen someone so confused in my life. It was almost comical.

"Did you love him right away? Like, at Thanksgiving?" His questions were spiraling, but I didn't mind as much anymore, since it was obvious he was just trying to get an understanding of what changed in his best friend.

I thought for a moment. "I think so. But I didn't know it right away. It was just so... confusing, I guess. I wasn't prepared to ever have those kinds of feelings for a guy, let alone someone my daughter was dating."

"So was it you and Jess with him from the beginning?" Greg asked.

"No..." I swallowed hard. "It was me and him first. Jess got involved later."

"You cheated on Jess with him?"

"Is this conversation going anywhere? Or are you getting off on making me relive painful memories?"

They both looked slightly taken aback. "Sorry, man. I was just curious, I guess..." Greg slugged back the rest of his drink.

"No, I'm sorry," I sighed. "I don't mean to get defensive. I just feel like we've been explaining ourselves to death, and it's getting a little frustrating. For the three of us it's easy. We just love each other, and nothing else matters. But everyone else wants answers to all these questions... It's been sort of draining."

Bill and Greg shared a look. Then Bill patted me hard on the back.

"It's alright, Lockwood. We get it. You fell for someone you never expected to fall for. I can't say it's happened to me, but I can understand it."

"Yea, and we support you. No matter what," Greg added with a smile.

"Thanks, guys." I grinned. "I appreciate it."

We went back to watching baseball... For about five minutes.

"So you're not attracted to us?" Bill asked, glancing at me.

A laugh of incredulity puffed from between my lips. *I should've known that wouldn't be the end of it. Someone kill me now.*

"No," I sighed, leaning my head back on the couch. "I'm not attracted to either of you."

"Why not?" Greg asked, sounding offended.

I laughed, "Because... I'm not?" I was still chuckling as I watched their faces, apparently having wounded their egos.

"I get it, I guess," Bill murmured. "I mean, look at the guy he's with."

I shot him an evil smirk. "You sure do make an awful lot of comments about how good-looking my husband is..."

"What are you insinuating?" He squinted at me.

"Nothing," I suppressed a grin, shrugging casually. "Just making an observation."

"Don't worry, Lockwood. I'm not trying to steal your man," Bill grumbled.

"Well, you never could. But thanks." I winked at him.

"What's it like having sex with a dude?" Greg blurted out.

I choked on air, and started coughing hysterically. "Are you fucking serious?!"

"Yea, which one of you... ya know... does the work...?" Bill wiggled his eyebrows and Greg fell onto his side with laughter.

"Oh dear Lord..." I covered my face with my hands. *Fucking buffoons, I'm telling you.*

Ryan picked the perfect moment to come strolling down the stairs, looking as chipper as ever. I was so glad he was feeling better. Seeing him happy was like a high I never wanted to come down from. *Now to ditch these morons so we can have some play time.*

"Ay! There's Mr. Lockwood!" Bill cheered through his chuckles. Greg saluted him.

Ryan's eyes danced between me and the drunk idiots. "What the hell is going on down here?"

"These dumbasses are asking me way too many personal questions about our sex life," I grinned, nodding him over.

He rounded the couch and leaned his butt up on the arm next to where I was sitting, hesitantly bringing his finger to trace the nape of my neck. I could tell he was still nervous about acting affectionately with me in front of people. We were so used to being in our own little bubble, tucked away inside the privacy of our home.

We hadn't been out of the house together much, aside from some shopping trips here and there. We ate dinner inside most nights, and hadn't gone out on many dates there in town. And I wanted to do all of those things with my husband and wife together. Now that everyone we loved knew about us, it was time we stopped hiding. We would need to get used to public displays of affection, not in a gross way. Just not shying away from little touches and stolen kisses every now and then.

It was slightly thrilling to think about.

With that in mind, I yanked Ryan onto my lap, scooting over a bit so he could sit next to me, pressed up against my side. I savored his warmth, and his smell, leaning in to kiss his jaw.

"What do you want to know?" Ryan sighed, grinning at my friends. I laughed softly.

Bill and Greg went quiet, staring at us with wide eyes. I had to laugh again.

"Oh, what's wrong?" My brow arched in teasing amusement. "I thought you had questions!"

"Yea, come on!" Ryan chuckled. "It's okay. I don't bite. Do I, baby?" Ryan swiveled his head in my direction.

"Sometimes," I growled low, eyeing him. "But I like it."

"Hm..." he hummed, moving in closer to my face until I could feel his breath on my lips. I kissed him slowly, and he nibbled my lower lip enough to send a shiver throughout my body.

"Alright, fine," I heard Bill grunt. "I have to admit, you guys are sort of cute together."

"Yea, man. Add Jess to the equation and you make a pretty adorable throuple." Greg added, shaking his head.

"Aw, thanks!" Ryan cheered softly, and I laughed. "So does this mean I get to be part of the group now?"

Greg and Bill shared a look. "Yea, sounds good to us."

"But we have more questions," Bill clapped his hands together. "I want to hear about Thailand."

I smiled and took Ryan's hand, threading my fingers through his.

Perfect.

JESSICA
Two Months After The Baby

I woke with a jolt, blinking over my sleepy eyes to check the baby monitor.

Ethan was sound asleep, and my pulse slowly steadied.

Looking around in the dark, it took my groggy mind a moment to realize what was off.

I was alone.

I was never alone in bed. I had two husbands, so our bed was always jam-packed with limbs, stiflingly hot muscley torsos and more often than not, morning wood. Or middle-of-the-night wood, because those things never seemed to go down.

Crawling out of bed, I decided to check on my baby, because seeing him through the monitor and physically touching his creamy soft skin were two totally different things.

I tip-toed around the corner into Ethan's nursery, creeping up to his crib as quietly as possible to catch a glimpse of the cutest damn baby on Earth. I was really trying not to make a peep, though, being that the last thing I wanted to do was wake an infant, and wind up listening to screaming because I couldn't keep my hands off for a couple more hours.

Peering over the edge of the crib at my son, my heart swelled so hard I thought my chest might fly open.

Our son is just the cutest, sweetest, most adorable baby there ever was. I'm sure of it.

I marveled at how truly perfect he was, lying there all quiet, his arm draped over his face. He slept like that most nights, which we all thought was hilarious and adorable. His little butt jutting out a bit in his ducky jammies.

I took a deep breath and held it, forcing myself to leave the room before I woke him up by accident. He'd be up in a couple hours to eat anyway, and jumping the gun would just serve to piss us both off.

I left the nursery, but stopped in front of my bedroom door.

Hmm...

If Ben and Ryan weren't in bed, I could only think of one other place they'd be. And being that it was almost two in the morning, the likelihood that they were in the basement, in Ben's man cave, was strong.

I gulped over my dry throat, a wave of curious excitement rushing through me.

See, I had just given birth two months ago. My sex drive was coming back in strides, but I hadn't actually had a dick in me since before Ethan was born. *Mouth doesn't count.*

Since I had two husbands, the sex was limitless. So even when I was slightly out of commission, my men were able to get their rocks off with each other. And I was totally fine with it.

For the most part.

Okay, sometimes I got a little jealous. But not of anything specific. I just wanted to have them toss me around like we were used to. But after having the baby, it couldn't really happen like that. The longer I stood in the hallway thinking, the more I began to convince myself that Ben and Ryan were hooking up downstairs, in lieu of something stupid like drinking beer and watching *Handmaid's Tale*.

What would be the harm in just checking on them? I mean, they're my husbands. And it's two a.m., and I woke up to an empty bed. So naturally I would go make sure they're alright...

My decision final, I sauntered down the stairs slowly, making my way to the basement. I breathed in deep as I opened the door, expecting to be hit with moans and grunts. But I didn't hear much of anything. The TV was definitely on, though. Maybe they were just watching shows and zoning out.

Ben didn't sleep well. It had certainly gotten better in the last year, but he still struggled with his sleep schedule. It was a blessing and a curse; the bad was that I hated him being exhausted, and loved falling asleep in his arms. But the good was that he had no problem getting up to feed or change Ethan at all hours since he wasn't usually asleep anyway.

Ryan, on the other hand, slept very well. Like a sexy log. But he too hated the thought of Ben up by himself struggling to get his needed rest. It wasn't unheard of for them to hang out in the man cave until Ben was tired enough to pass out.

I took the stairs down into the basement, and sure enough as I grew closer, I could hear something that sent a shiver across my chest, hardening my nipples something fierce.

They were kissing. It was an obvious sound, especially since they were both amazing kissers and the lip-sucking noises were always accompanied by soft little pants and gasps, from all of us.

Peering around the corner at the couch, I was desperate to get a look at my two hot-as-all-fuck husbands, and their little make-out session. My heart was already thudding inside my ribcage at the idea of spying on them. Between my thighs was growing more slippery by the second.

"Mmm..."

My eyes were wide as I watched my husbands kissing. Ben was holding Ryan's jaw, owning the fuck out of his mouth while Ryan's hands slinked down over Ben's broad shoulders and defined chest. I wasn't exactly right next to them, but I was close enough to see everything they were doing over the top of the couch. They were both wearing only pajama pants; typical nighttime attire. And it looked *awesome*.

"I love your hands on me," Ben whispered, before touching his tongue to Ryan's. My clit throbbed.

"Where should I touch you next, my sexy ass husband?" Ryan grinned and tugged Ben's lip slowly between his teeth.

"Wherever you want, baby," Ben purred in a tone that made me drip even more. "I'm yours."

"Mmm... I love how that sounds," Ryan growled, pushing on Ben's chest until he was on top of him, and my view was obstructed by the back of the couch.

Dammit! I need to see this. I'm so hard-up right now. It feels like it's been an eternity since I got laid. I want to watch...

I never actually got to see Ben and Ryan together in their own bubble. Sure, I watched them together while we were all messing around, but it was different when it was the three of us. At that moment, with them blissfully unaware of their secret audience, I could witness the lust and desire; the passion they had for one another.

It was hot as hell, knowing they had that kind of connection. It was the same connection I had with Ben, and Ryan. We had chemistry together as couples, and as a trio. But watching them vibe on each other alone was a whole other point of arousal.

I wasn't an overly jealous girl, because before Ryan, Ben

had always been hopelessly devoted to only me. Of course I got annoyed watching girls hit on him, but only when they did it in a blatant, slutty way. When girls giggled and flipped their hair for him, I found it kind of funny and cute. My husband was an unstoppable force, and you'd have to be deaf and blind and living in another state not to notice him.

Ryan was still a relatively new part of our world, so we were still learning about, and growing into our feelings for him. I didn't get crazy jealous over watching girls, and guys, flirt with him either. Again, because he only had eyes for us, so it really didn't matter.

Still, you'd think watching your husband hooking up with someone who wasn't you would give you that suffocating feeling of jealousy, crawling through your chest and squeezing your lungs. But that certainly wasn't happening now. All I could feel were my inner walls tightening, and my panties soaking through.

Deciding to act on impulse, I step closer to them so I could keep watching. I stayed as quiet as possible, sticking to the edge of the room where it was darkest, moving up to the side of the pool table, where I had a perfect view of the couch and neither of them could see me. They probably *could* have, if they were paying attention. But Ryan was grinding his hips on Ben's and they were kissing mercilessly, so clearly they weren't on the lookout out for voyeurs.

"You like this, baby?" Ryan hummed, stroking his clothed hard-on against Ben's.

They were so hard I could actually see their erections through their clothes from where I was standing. Plus, they both had huge dicks, so that helped.

I am the luckiest girl on Earth. Both my husbands are packing nine-plus inches. Go me.

I licked my lips as Ben pushed Ryan's pants down around

his ass. Ryan's cock flopped out onto Ben's six-pack and I seriously almost came just from the *sound* it made, because *holy fuck* what kind of dick actually made that noise when it hit something?! And Ben's abs were like stones beneath his smooth golden skin, so it worked out perfectly.

Lord, have mercy. This is fire.

"Ryan..." Ben panted, grabbing our husband's cock in his big, strong hand, jerking it slowly. "Fuck, I want you in my mouth."

"Yea?" Ryan mewled, sounding like he was losing his bearings a bit, which he probably was. Seeing how turned on he was by Ben was euphoric. "You want to suck my hard dick with those luscious lips?"

"Mhm..." Ben nodded, moving his soft kisses across Ryan's jaw and down his throat. "Fuck my mouth, baby."

Ryan pulled back, his chest heaving with rapid breaths as he removed his pants completely, kneeling over Ben's torso. He stroked his long dick with his hand, up and down, right in front of Ben's mouth, and I was shivering with anticipation. I watched their faces closely, eyes locked on one another's, sharing the same telepathic thoughts, which I too could understand because we were *that* connected.

You look so fucking good right now.

I love you. I love your body.

I want to control you; make you tremble with pleasure.

You're mine.

Ryan let go of himself and took Ben's jaw in his palm, moving in closer, dragging the head of his cock over Ben's lower lip.

I chomped on mine to stay quiet.

Ben parted his lips, opening up and extending his tongue just enough so that Ryan could slide his dick into Ben's mouth.

He pushed a bit, feeding inches between Ben's lips while Ben hollowed his cheeks and sucked on the crown.

"God damn..." Ryan moved in more, thrusting himself in and out of Ben's mouth, fucking like he would either of our holes. It looked so mind-numbingly good, I almost couldn't process it.

Ben groaned softly, sucking more while Ryan shoved his cock into the back of Ben's throat. Ben didn't even flinch, which had me grinning to myself. *He's getting really good at blowjobs. That's my man.*

Ryan's hips developed a rhythm as he pumped himself between Ben's lips, fully fucking his throat while gripping the nape of Ben's neck, holding him in place. Then I noticed that Ryan's other hand was behind him, inside Ben's pajamas, jerking his dick off while he rode his face.

At that point, I really couldn't help myself. Sliding my hand between my thighs, I swirled my fingers over the wet material of my panties. I bit my lip harder to stifle the moans that wanted to escape me as I touched myself, watching my husbands do very dirty things to each other.

God, this is too fucking good. I love watching them. It's like live action porn.

"Ben, holy fuck," Ryan gasped, lolling his head back. "Swallow my cock, baby. Jesus, your mouth is so warm and wet and fucking perfect. I love you, baby... I love... you... *fuck*, harder!"

Ben's eyes were glossy and his cheeks were flushed. I could feel him burning up from where I was standing, craving their orgasms as much my own, my mind desperate to watch Ryan come in Ben's mouth.

But suddenly he stilled, tugging himself from between Ben's lips, leaving his giant, engorged erection slick with Ben's saliva. Ben gave Ryan a desperate look, which brought on a tremor of my walls. I was so wet I could feel it coating my inner thighs.

I need to get fucked tonight. No more waiting. This is happening.

Ryan repositioned himself, ripping Ben's pants down fast then kneeling between his parted thighs. Ben bent his knees as Ryan moved over him, kissing his lips hard, a clear hunger showering his entire body. He kissed down Ben's neck and chest, sucking on his nipples, toying with them until Ben moaned out loud.

Then he made his way south, licking Ben's abs before taking him in his mouth. I saw Ben shudder, his dick visibly flinching between Ryan's lips. Ryan trailed onto Ben's balls, kissing and tonguing them, grabbing his ass with both hands and lifting his hips a bit.

Swallowing hard, I bit my lip until it bled, the taste of copper in my mouth turning me on even more. My body was vibrating; pulsing with need. Everything I was watching was threatening to unravel me completely.

Ryan spread Ben open, wasting no time licking between his cheeks, grunting as he went, eating Ben's ass out with such fervor I could feel it myself. He had such a skilled mouth. His tongue worked wonders on my lady parts, and it was doing just the same to my husband's ass. I whimpered, but caught myself before I let the sound slip.

What would they do if they saw me right now?

"Fuck, Ryan..." Ben stroked his cock slowly while Ryan kissed and bit his ass, Ben's legs wrapping around Ryan's shoulders to pull him closer. "That feels so good... oh *God,* eat me, baby..."

"How bad do you want me balls deep in you right now?" Ryan growled, raising his brow.

I almost fell over. My legs were like jelly.

"So bad, baby," Ben groaned, gazing down at our husband between his legs. "Fill my ass with your thick cock. *Please...*"

A stuttered squeak flew from inside my throat, and I instantly slapped my hand over my mouth.

But it was too late.

Ryan's eyes lifted, and he squinted before realizing that I was standing there. With my hand in my panties.

Ben must have heard as well, and caught on to what Ryan was seeing, because he swiveled his head to look behind him at the pool table. His eyes met mine, and we stared at one another for a beat, his chest still moving up and down with forceful breaths.

I shifted my eyes back to Ryan and he grinned, tugging his lip between his teeth. I looked to Ben again, and he raised his brow at me. They both looked so painfully good, I could feel the crackle between my thighs. Their hair was all mussed up, both of their faces flushed, sweat glistening on the sinews of their muscled bodies. I couldn't remember ever being so turned on in my entire life.

"I didn't realize we had an audience," Ben rasped, licking his lips.

"What are you doing over there, wife?" Ryan's voice came out low and tempting, dripping sweet like honeycomb.

"I..." My voice gave out as I stammered. "I'm... I..."

My face was like an oven. They were both just staring at me, waiting for me to explain myself, or do something, but I couldn't. I was frozen.

"This can play out however you want, Mrs. Lockwood-Harper," Ben rumbled, his brilliant blue eyes sparkling. "We can give you the rest of the show... or you can participate in it."

"Choice is yours, beautiful," Ryan added, his hands casually caressing Ben's ass and thighs.

Ben's eyes drooped shut and he purred out a sweet sound. "Jess..."

I gulped and my fingers twitched, rubbing my clit in slow circles.

"Mmm... Jessica..." Ryan hummed then ran his tongue along the length of Ben's twinging cock. "So good..."

I moaned softly, sliding my panties down and slipping Ben's t-shirt over my head. My breasts were still huge and swollen from the breastfeeding, my nipples peaked and ready to be touched.

"Come join us, baby," Ben pleaded, his eyes back on mine.

I whimpered and finally moved my feet, walking on shaky legs over to the couch. They both sat up and I scooted in between them. But before I knew what was happening, Ben scooped me into his arms and laid me down beneath him. He and Ryan both moved over me, kissing each other and then kissing me.

The feeling of both their lips at the same time was lethal. Ben kissed my mouth while Ryan kissed my neck, then they each found one of my tits and began simultaneously lapping at my nipples like candy. My breasts were sensitive, but it felt so amazing I could barely breathe. I dug my fingers into both of their hair, ripping at the strands while they sucked my hardened peaks.

Ben chuckled deviously, opening his eyes to look at Ryan. "Do you taste it?" His voice was so low, I had barely heard him.

Ryan nodded. "Mmm... *Fuck*, that's hot."

They left my tits feeling bereft as they moved down my body together, nipping everywhere their warm mouths could reach. Finally they arrived at the apex of my thighs and gave each other another look. I simply watched in fascination. *This is the most incredible thing that's ever happened.*

They peppered my inner thighs with kisses, then Ryan

grabbed Ben's face, pulling him into a sensual kiss that had me melting everywhere, and it wasn't even me who was being kissed. Their lips moved together, tongues advancing as I watched in awe. Then they pulled apart, all three of us breathless, and lowered their heads to my pussy.

This was the first time I'd let them eat me out since I had the baby, but there were no hesitations. A blissful completeness washed over me as both of their mouths kissed and sucked different spots on my tender, soaking wet flesh. Their joined tongues extended, licking my clit, my lips, each other. It was like they were kissing each other and my pussy at the same time, and it became an overload to my body.

I had never felt anything so intense and spectacular in my life. Two sets of lips, sucking everywhere; two tongues, gliding and tracing, slipping inside me and torturing me with their rhythm. I spread my legs as wide as I could, ignoring the nagging want to stretch out long. Ben's hands massaged my tits while Ryan gripped my thigh, forcing me open for them.

"You taste like candy," he moaned, his breath sending me soaring.

"Sweet..." Ben's voice vibrated into me. "So fucking sweet."

I couldn't hold out any longer. I gasped out loud, lifting my hips to meet their mouths as the strongest orgasm I'd ever felt ripped through my body. I shook and quaked down to my core as I climaxed so hard, my pussy pulsing juices all over their lips.

I was buzzing in an orb of pleasure. As I came down, Ben wrapped me up in his arms, the unmistakable feeling of his rock-solid erection resting between us. I peeled my eyes open to see what they were doing.

Ryan was behind Ben, kissing his neck and shoulders, holding his ass in two handfuls. Ben pressed his forehead down on mine, planting a soft kiss on my lips.

"Hi, gorgeous," he murmured, flicking his hips to drag his cock through my wetness. "How do you feel?"

"Amazing..." I whimpered, holding his face in my hands. "Ben... I love you..."

"I love you too, baby," his voice rumbled as he took his cock in his hand, pressing it up to my entrance. "Are you ready?"

I knew what he meant. He was asking if I was ready to be fucked for the first time since the baby.

My answer was an emphatic, "Fuck *yes*."

He growled out a sexy chuckle, kissing my jaw as he began to push inside me.

I was so focused on the feeling; the incredible, intense sensation of being filled by him for the first time in a while, that I almost didn't notice him moaning out loud into the crook of my neck.

Because Ryan was pushing into him at the same time, filling Ben's ass up with his big dick.

Oh fuck... My God, I'm going to erupt again so soon. I don't stand a chance with these two!

I cried out as Ben forced his thick, aching cock inside me almost all the way, the natural lubrication from my arousal and tidal wave climax making it much easier for him to move. Then he drew his hips back, popping his butt against Ryan's hips, sliding the other giant dick deep inside himself.

Ben and Ryan worked up a tempo, moving together. Ryan stroked into Ben's tightness while Ben pumped into mine, then they went back. It was like a rocking chair, moving slow, yet steady, both of their hips working together so the three of us could fuck so good I was going cross-eyed.

My hands were everywhere. On Ben's chest and abs, his hips, his ass; holding him open for Ryan. *Jesus*... It was so dirty and bad, but still the hottest damn thing I had ever done. I wrapped my legs around both of them, reaching for Ryan's ass to pull him deeper into both of us. I was overflowing with need, my next orgasm brimming at the surface.

We were all groaning and panting, growling and cursing and screaming each other's names until our throats were hoarse.

Fuck... Fuck fuck fuuuuck this is fantastic.

"Fuck, I'm gonna come again..." I croaked, grasping Ryan's hand and holding it on Ben's waist. "I'm gonna come on your cock, Ben."

"Please do..." he whimpered, dropping his face to my tits, licking and sucking everywhere while being pounded. "Oh God... that feels... *yes*. Right there... *Yessss, baby*..."

"Is Ryan's dick hitting your spot?" I mewled, my walls tightening on his stroking shaft as he grazed my spot over and over.

"Mhm," he nodded fast, sweat dripping down his glorious muscles.

"Ryan... Are you gonna come in your husband's ass?" I squealed, letting go.

"Yes... Fuck!" Ryan roared, the sound of his hips smacking against Ben's behind sending me right over the edge.

I erupted into a tornado of an orgasm, screaming out their names, sucking and biting all over Ben's neck and shoulder. Ryan grabbed my hip and held onto me while he found his own release inside Ben.

"Fuck, baby, you feel so good... I'm coming in your sweet ass, Ben... Jesus, I fucking love you."

"I'm gonna pull out," Ben grunted, sliding his dick out of me fast, stroking himself hard with my juices. "Ryan, stay... in me... *fuck!*"

Ryan held Ben close to him while he came, shooting his hot come all over my pussy, stomach and tits. It was so amazingly naughty; filthy, wild and wonderful. I couldn't keep my eyes off.

The world finally stopped spinning as we all cuddled in a giant mass of limbs, kissing and touching each other like fiends.

Until the sound of a crying baby broke through our post-orgasm trance.

I glanced up in brief panic at the second baby monitor that Ben kept with him downstairs. Ethan was up and rolling around, throwing his little hands in the air, ready for his nightly feeding.

"Wow," Ben chuckled, still recovering his breath. "Perfect timing."

"I know, tell me about it," Ryan giggled, brushing Ben's sweaty hair back with his fingers. "The kid definitely gets rewarded for giving mommy and daddies their play time."

I laughed softly, kissing his shoulder and neck, then Ben's chest.

My heart was stuffed full. I had never been so overflowing with bliss, there were actually tears running down my cheeks.

"Hey... You okay?" Ryan asked, taking my chin in his fingers. Ben watched me closely, playing with my hair.

"I'm... so happy."

They both grinned at me and replied, "Me too."

PULL

A PUSH NOVELLA, PRESENTS...

Pride

CHAPTER ONE
Ryan

I t's rainbow overload!

My eyes are tugged in every direction, like a cat being distracted by shiny objects.

Flags, signs, costumes, wigs, glitter and sparkles... *Oh, the sparkles.*

"Everything is so sparkly!" I gasp, grinning at the guy who's grinning at me, wearing only some itty bitty shorts and glitter galore smeared all over his tanned muscles.

"Alright alright," Ben grumbles, pulling me closer to him, practically swallowing me up with his giant arms to protect me from the prying eyes of hot dudes.

Hot dudes everywhere. This is amazing.

And a little overwhelming. But, like, in a good way.

I feel like I belong here.

We're in Albuquerque for our first ever Pride Parade. We decided to make it a weekend trip, booked a hotel and brought Ethan. It's the cutest thing in the world, seeing his little face light up from all the excitement as Jess pushes him in his stroller.

He has a non-toxic rainbow stamp on his chubby little

cheek, and Jess made him the most adorable onesie that says, *My parents went queer and all I got was this onesie.* I think I laughed so hard I burst into tears when she showed it to me the other day.

She also made shirts for us, and one for herself that says *I'm with them* in rainbows, two arrows made of the Poly flag colors pointing in each direction.

"Babe, you gotta loosen up just a smidge," Jessica says to Ben, pulling us off to the side of the bustling sidewalk so she can adjust Ethan's hat. It's hot as balls out today, and we decided Jess would bring Ethan out for a few just to introduce him to Pride before adjourning to the air conditioned hotel room. "This is such a big thing. For *both* of you. You need to get the full experience."

"Meaning I need to just stand back and let my husband be ogled by strange men?" Ben gives our wife a look before taking a gulp from his bottle of water.

"Yea, kind of," she shrugs with a grin.

Ben hands me the bottle and I finish it off. "I love that you think I'm getting ogled more than you are," I chuckle when he aims that frumpy scowl in my direction.

I also love how he thinks it still intimidates me the same way it did last year... When we did something we weren't supposed to, and it somehow turned into the most beautiful thing I could ever know.

Ben blinks at me, apparently considering my words before he glances left, then right. There are a lot of eyes on him at the moment, all deserving, of course. He looks good—*damn good*—as he always does. But today in particular, wearing his sleeveless *Why Choose?* shirt decorated in Pan & Poly colors. I'm wearing something similar, but for some reason on Ben it just looks... life-affirming.

He's mine. He's *ours*... A thought worth drooling over.

"The arms on you, though," another barely-dressed dude sighs as he walks by us, eye fucking the shit out of my husband so hard I almost double over with laughter.

"This is amazing," I wrap my arms around his waist and pepper his jaw with kisses, earning us a few *awww*'s from nearby onlookers—who are everywhere, by the way. The streets are packed with people, all decked out in drag, leather and lace and fishnet and rainbows, as far as the eye can see.

I'm just loving this so hard.

"Okay, well I don't really care about the attention of all these people," Ben sighs, letting his hand drift down to my ass. Then the *awww*'s change to a few *alright, get a room*'s. "In case you haven't noticed, I'm mainly here for you, baby."

Gazing up at his perfectly chiseled face, I bite my lip. "And I couldn't be more appreciative. But I want you to enjoy yourself, too. It's like Jess said, we need to have this experience. It's like losing your virginity."

A deep laugh bubbles from his throat and I can't help but press my thumb to his lower lip.

"I lost my virginity to you," he mumbles, holding me close with his lips drifting over to my ear. "In a sense..."

"Best day ever," I grin while feeling him up just enough and knowing this is one place where I never *ever* have to worry about people judging us.

It's not something I worry about much as it is. I fell pretty easily into uncovering my bisexuality, and I consider myself insanely fortunate that everyone in my life is so supportive. Millions of others haven't been so lucky, and that's the other reason I wanted to come today.

If me showing up can let even just one person know it's okay to love who you want to love, to stand up as a guy and say *I kissed a boy and I liked it*, then this is exactly where I need to be on this lovely, albeit scorching, June afternoon.

A cute little whine that I'm choosing to interpret as *Dada* tugs me away from my sexy ass husband and I turn back toward Jess and Ethan in the stroller.

"He wants you, babe," Jess tells me, lifting him out so I can swing him around.

My heart has never been fuller than it is today, and having Ethan here is the final thing to stuff it up. My son is the best kid who's ever existed. *I know every parent says that, but in our case it's true!* I never knew how awesome being a dad could feel until this unexpected little peanut came along.

Ethan's about nine months old—we'll be celebrating his first birthday in only a few more months and I can't wait. Jess and I are already talking about a big party.

"What do you think, kiddo?" I ask Ethan, as if he'll answer me. "You wanna go check out the parade?"

He squeals something that I'll take as a *yes*, and we pick back up walking, making our way through the crowd toward the cheering bystanders. People move aside for us so we can get Ethan closer, everyone smiling and commenting on how adorable he is, and of course on the epic onesie he's in. Jess takes a bow for that one.

It is indeed epic.

We watch the parade for a bit, the floats huge and decorated to the fullest in color. I love how beautiful it all is, the love. Love for each other, and for ourselves. It's so powerful, I can feel it in the air.

The struggle to finding yourself is one that can take a while, and sometimes feel hopeless. All these people, whether they get to be themselves every day of the year, or only today, they're the bravest damn people ever. *Such an incredible celebration.*

Ben presses a kiss to my cheek, and I smile when Jess wraps

her arm around my waist, resting her head on my shoulder. *What a great day.*

Once we're done watching the parade, and I can feel Ethan getting restless, we decide to walk back toward the hotel.

"You sure you don't mind taking him back?" Ben asks, concern lining his eyes for our wife. "This isn't just about us, you know." He means him and me.

Jess and I had talked about it. She voiced her concerns about not wanting to interfere with Ben and my celebrations. But I assured her that celebrating Poly pride is just as important. She's married to queer guys, after all. Doesn't get much closer than that.

"I know it's not," she tells Ben, holding their joined hands up to her heart. "I had an amazing day. Bringing Ethan here to witness all this... It's more than I could ever ask for." She gives him an assuring smile, then turns to me quickly.

I just wink at her. Jess and I are simpatico. We always have been. I tend to understand where she's coming from, because so often the ways she thinks and reacts are ways I would do the same. She's the best wife two guys could ever ask for because she recognizes that we each need to have our own relationships, outside of the throuple. She and Ben have their thing, the most solid connection I've ever encountered. She and I have our thing, too.

And then there's me and Ben...

Fireworks on steroids. Intensity and chemistry, like fire on fire.

Jess gets that, and she loves it. Jealousy is a part of what we do. Recognizing it and loving it too has been the biggest accomplishment in this marriage. We're solid.

And we just so happen to be celebrating our one-year anniversary next weekend. *I can't wait.*

Ben hugs Jess hard and gives her a kiss that takes *my* breath away, and I'm not even on the receiving end. Then he cuddles Ethan a hundred times, while I give Jess some love of my own.

"Order room service," I tell her with my lips in her soft blonde hair that smells like vanilla heaven on earth. "Take advantage of that huge Jacuzzi bathtub."

"Oooh memories," she purrs next to my ear and it makes my dick move.

I have to give her a little tap on the ass.

Then I say goodbye to my son before Jess straps him back into the stroller, waving at us as she makes her way back into the hotel.

Ben and I take a synchronized sigh before turning back to one another. Our eyes are wide and alit with excitement. Eagerness, for all the possibilities.

"So... what should we do?" He asks, eyes falling to my mouth. It zips a chill up my spine.

"Not what you're thinking," I chuckle, and he pouts. "Not *yet*, I mean."

"Tell me what you want, baby," he hums, pressing himself into me until I'm wishing our clothes would just disintegrate off our bodies, "And I'll make it happen."

Taking his hand in mine, I pull him with me, mainly just to get us off the street before we end up arrested for public indecency. "Let's get a drink."

"'Kay..." he breathes, that rumbly voice of his doing nothing to stop me from becoming rock hard.

I have to focus. *No boners in public.* Though glancing at our surrounding company, I'm not sure anyone would care, or even notice.

All the restaurants and bars have rainbow flags hanging up outside, decor on the windows, their doors wide open with people mulling about. Everything is just so packed. I've never seen the city like this, and it's awesome. I yank Ben into a place

I've been to once or twice, called The Quirk. Immediately a great decision because it's dark and cool in here, and according to the chalkboards on the walls, there are endless options for Pride-themed drinks.

Ben scoots up to the bar and I nestle in next to him, between the crowd of loud and proud people. It's mostly guys, but there are a few females scattered amongst them. The ratio is crazy. Let's just say there's a lot of testosterone in the room.

"Scotch, please," Ben starts saying to the bartender, but I hold my hand up to stop him.

"He'll have the Penis Colada," I grin, feeling Ben's grimace on the side of my face. "Make it two."

"Coming right up, sweetheart," the bartender croons, then wanders off to make our drinks.

I'm assuming, based on the name, it's the one with a phallic-shaped banana creation sticking out the top that everyone in here seems to be enjoying.

"Ryan," Ben grumbles, but then his broody face is swept up into a dazzling *Ben Lockwood* smile.

"Yes, darling?" I lean up on the bar, awaiting whatever it is he needs to say.

He simply lets out a long breath laced with a little chuckle. "I fucking love you."

His hands appear on my waist and he pulls me flush against the solid wall of his chest, making it so easy for me to drape my arms around his wide shoulders and play with his dirty blonde hair at the nape of his neck.

"Love was never like this before you," I murmur over his lips, then I kiss him.

I kiss him because he's my husband, and I love him unlike anything I could possibly comprehend. The most awakening shock to my system was falling in love with Ben.

And I'll never look back.

Ben kisses me back hard, with the part of him that's never been shy about showing me affection in public. He kisses me exactly the same way when we're in the middle of a crowded room that he does when we're alone. Like he *loves* me. Like he, too, can't believe he has *me*.

It's mesmerizing.

"I want you so bad right now, baby," he whispers, tone spritzed with that rare Ben vulnerability that makes him like a zillion times sexier. His curious fingers slink around to my front, tracing the muscles beneath my tank top. "I wanna lick you everywhere."

I laugh into his mouth. "Like a lollipop?"

"Mhmm..." he nods, brushing his lips over mine. "You're so damn sexy, Ryan. I still can't believe I get to have you." He pulls back so we can make eye contact, his shimmering blue holding me in place. "I can't believe we're here... Married and like... *here*. This is—"

"Fabulous?" I smirk and he laughs out loud before stopping himself to force a scowl.

"Stop being such a wise ass, kid," he trails his hot mouth down my neck. "Or you won't get all the licking."

"Oh, but I need the licking," I mumble through my persistent grin.

"I know you do." His tongue makes a small circle on my pulse point and I shiver in his arms. "I wanna eat you like a banana *split*."

"Jesus fucking Christ..." I hum, practically falling into him. But then my eyes catch sight of the massive, elaborately ridiculous drinks the bartender just delivered us. "Speaking of bananas..."

Ben leaves my neck alone and needy to peer at our drinks. His brow arches and he stares at them for a solid five seconds in silence before he turns that grouchy glare on me.

"I'm not drinking that," he says, fully serious.

I have to laugh out loud, picking up my drink, which is essentially a frozen Pina colada, only it's rainbow colored and there's a banana hanging out of it with a half-lime sitting atop, like a nice crown... The drink is complete with a rainbow flag and a penis straw. Hence... *Penis* Colada, apparently.

The thing is nuts. *Literally*. I immediately snap a picture of it with my phone to commemorate the experience.

"Babe, you have to drink it." I pick up the fruit penis, examining it closely.

When my eyes come back to Ben, the look he's giving me is priceless. Part unamused Ben, part nervous former straight guy at his first Pride celebration being faced with a penis drink.

It's the cutest damn thing I've ever seen in my life.

"For me?" I give him the puppy dog eyes and he rolls his, picking up the drink.

Bringing the straw to his lips, he takes a nice long pull from the penis. I bite my lip, watching as he swallows, Adam's apple sliding in that delicious, stubble-clad throat of his.

I stare at him, and him back at me, for a quiet moment until he finally whispers, "It's delicious."

I can't help bursting out into more laughter while I take pictures of him.

We both sip our ridiculous drinks, making the sex eyes at each other the entire time, while I consider how cliché it would be to drag him into the bathroom and utilize one of the little packets of banana-flavored lube that apparently comes with the drink.

It's only happy hour, and I can tell from how loose everyone's already getting in here that tonight is going to be wild. And I'm excited to experience it. I've never been to a gay club. I've never danced with Ben in public and I think it's something

I would love to do. There's a lot I'd love to do with him, actually. And we have the rest of our lives to do it...

The thought is enthralling.

"You need to stop looking at me like that," Ben pulls me into him with his index finger in the belt loop of my shorts.

"And why would that be, oh husband of mine?" I play coy, obsessed with the fire he's shooting at me through his burning blue eyes.

"Because I'm two seconds from dragging you into that bathroom." He nods toward the back of the bar.

"Funny," I lick my lip, touching his chest slowly, "I was just thinking the exact same thing."

Ben growls, eyes set on my mouth, before he sets his drink down. "Let's go."

"Where are we going?" I tease with a love drunk grin on my face.

"I'm ready for my next drink," he whispers, and I'm fucking *dying*.

Ben tosses cash onto the bar then grabs me by the arm, rather forcefully, sending a zap of excitement to my gut as he yanks me along toward the bathroom. As we reach the corridor to the men's room, he stops short when we practically crash right into someone.

"Oh... hello there, Lockwoods."

My eyes turn to the man, widening as I hear Ben mutter, "You've gotta be fucking kidding me."

And I swallow hard. "Hi, Tate."

CHAPTER TWO
Ben

Wow, what a buzzkill.

Nothing like running into your husband's ex-fling at your first Pride celebration, huh?

What are the odds?

Sure, I know Tate lives in New Mexico, and this is the biggest parade for Pride in the state. But honestly, of all the bars...

The only other guy Ryan's hooked up with, and here the fuck he is, smirking at me like he's in on something I'm not. I fucking *hate* that look. Last time I saw it, I was punching it off his smug prick face.

We sort of buried the hatchet since then, but that doesn't mean we're anxious to hang out. At least, I'm not.

Ryan on the other hand, my sweet husband who doesn't have a mean bone in his perfect body, isn't having the same reaction as me. He's wearing an easy smile as he gives Tate a hug which goes on for three excruciating seconds. I'm literally about to pull them apart.

"Good to see you," Ryan murmurs, his cheeks a little

flushed, likely from the strong as hell drinks we just killed, and the fact that we were clearly about to sneak off for dirty activities in the restroom.

"You too, Harper," Tate says, eyes bouncing back and forth between us.

"It's Harper-Lockwood now." Ryan holds up his left hand to display the platinum band on his ring finger.

I love seeing it... It makes me want to kiss him everywhere so badly. And this douchebag is interrupting it.

"Right," Tate hums. "How could I forget? So, here for your first Pride parade, hm?"

Ryan nods, still sucking on the penis straw of his drink I thought he'd left behind. Tate's eyes go to Ryan's mouth, and it takes every ounce of strength in my body not to pluck them out of his skull.

"Look, Tate, it's been great catching up, but we were just leaving," I tug Ryan by his belt loops again, and he sort of stumbles with me, like a puppy who's got a nice buzz going.

"Oh yea, I'm sure you were leaving through the men's room," Tate chuckles sarcastically. "It's Pride, Lockwood. No shame in getting some action in bathrooms. I mean, been there done that. Right, Ryan?"

Ryan's face pales as his green eyes jump to mine, wide and unblinking. I'm sure he thinks I'm going to punch Tate in the face for that comment. And if it were a year ago, maybe I would have. Okay, I *definitely* would have.

But now, this man is my husband. He's wearing my ring on his finger, and my last name attached to his. There's no need for any of this back and forth catty shit, and Tate's just trying to get a rise out of me anyway.

Which reminds me...

"Actually, it's Lockwood-*Harper* now." I pull the fakest grin I possess, showing off my second wedding band as I slink my left arm around my husband's waist. "And now that I think about it, the bathroom's probably sorta crowded. We could always go back to the suite, right babe?"

"I'll go anywhere with you," Ryan breathes out like he's suddenly sleepy as he nestles up to me, leaning his weight on my side. "Damn, those drinks are *really* strong..."

I peer at him in between mirroring Tate's smug smirk. "You're not supposed to chug it in two seconds, kid."

"So affectionate when he's drunk," Tate sneers.

"Yea well," my jaw clenches in hopes I can control the rage bubbling inside me, "It's a celebration. We haven't gone out in a while, what with the baby."

"Right, the *baby*." Tate's grin grows a little less forced. "How is Ethan? And Jessica! Is she here?" He starts looking around.

"She's at the hotel with Ethan," I tell him, distracted by Ryan kissing my neck and trying to stuff his hand down my pants. "It's hot as balls outside and he was getting kind of cranky—babe! Jesus."

Ryan starts giggling like a drunk fool. And then I remember I was supposed to make sure he ate before drinking since he's a damn lightweight. But apparently, he was too excited about the parade to be concerned with food.

"Well, again it was great catching up, Tate, but I have to get my husband something to eat before he passes out," I tell Tate while trying to extract Ryan's hand from inside my boxers.

"Hey, I'm actually going to a party right now at a friend's house around the corner," Tate says, pleasantly enough, though who would know. "There'll be plenty of food if you guys want to join."

"I don't think—"

"That sounds awesome!" Ryan cheers. "Babe, a Pride party! Doesn't that sound awesome??"

I blink at him, trying really hard to get him to read my thoughts. *Baby, I know you're a little tipsy right now, but I have no earthly desire to hang out with Tate and his friends. Please don't make me do this.*

He gapes at me for a moment, and for a split second I think maybe he *is* hearing me.

But then he leans in close to my ear and whispers, "Fucking at the party will be *way* more fun than fucking in the bathroom, don't you think?" He extends his tongue to swipe the shell of my ear before sucking the lobe between his lips.

My dick is all too ready to oblige.

Clearing my throat, I glance at Tate. "Around the corner?"

Tate's friend's house is super nice.

It's a sort of townhouse type with a backyard patio area, which is where everyone is hanging out. I immediately smell the grilling food and while it's making my stomach rumble up a storm, I'm more concerned with getting something into Ryan's so he doesn't get sick.

Sick, though, is not how he seems. He seems like he's having the time of his life, waving at strangers and shimmying to the thumping Lady Gaga playing over the seemingly giant speakers I don't see anywhere.

Another thing about this party: It's ninety-eight percent dudes.

I spot two females. *Two.* Honestly, they're hard to miss in this crowd of half-dressed men, all of whom are in amazing shape.

Pride is something I never anticipated myself attending before last year, and yet now that I'm here, I'm sort of liking it.

Begrudgingly. Like, I wouldn't broadcast that I'm having a good time, but it *is* fun to be in this sort of setting, although I'd still much rather be at home in the man-cave with my family. *I'm a homebody, okay?*

Not even necessarily at *home*, but I prefer to spend time alone with my partners. This seems like fun once a year, but I haven't been a party animal since I was in high school. I'm not going back to it now that I'm nearing forty.

Ryan, on the other hand... He's still so young. That's what worries me on occasion; that he's giving up youthful experiences to settle in with Jess and me. He's never alluded to it, and he always shuts me down when I bring it up, but I can't help the insecurities.

So, more than anything, this is for him.

The measures I'd take to make this kid happy know no bounds. Clearly, since looking around I don't exactly feel like I fit in here. But I suppose my husband is my VIP pass into the Pride setting?

I have no idea...

"Hey there," a shirtless guy with giant sunglasses and a rainbow bandana tied around his head comes up to us, kisses Tate on the cheek and hands Ryan a drink. Ryan goes to immediately take a sip, but I snatch it away from him. "I'm so happy to see you, love." He's talking to Tate. Then his face tilts in our direction. "Who are your friends? They're yummy."

"Kennan, this is Ben and his husband, Ryan," Tate introduces us. "Ben and I grew up together." Then he tells us, "This is Ken's house."

I nod, shaking his hand. "Thanks for having us."

"Can't say no to more eye candy on Pride." He flashes a bight grin. "Especially of the *Daddy* variety."

I purse my lips while Ryan giggles.

"Ryan here needs to eat before he ends up snoring," Tate tells his friend, then motions toward the grill.

"Oh please, knock yourselves out," Kennan offers politely. "There's way more than enough food since half these queens won't be eating." He lets out an exuberant laugh to which Tate grins. But it stops abruptly when he gasps, "*Ryan?! Is this the one...?*"

Kennan's head tilts in the direction of my husband, though he seems to be sharing some unspoken words with Tate. Tate nods and Kennan lowers his sunglasses to get a good look at Ryan.

"Okay, that's enough," I drag my husband away while the two of them laugh amongst themselves. "Assholes," my jaw tightens, and I deposit Ryan on a chair, grabbing a plate of grilled chicken and potato salad and sliding it in front of him. "Eat."

"Why are you so grumpy?" He pouts, but does as I say, taking the tiniest bites ever.

"It's annoying," I sigh, fisting my hair.

"What is?"

"The fact that you hooked up with him..." I mutter petulantly. "Multiple times. I actually fucking hate it."

"Yea, I'm aware," he says, though his lips are curving into a content little smirk.

I glare at him. "Why does that make you happy?"

"Because... I *love* that you're jealous," he tells me, reaching out to run his fingers over mine on the table. "I've always loved your possessiveness. I don't know why, but it just... It lets me know how you feel. Even before, when you didn't tell me."

Swallowing hard, I stare at him while he chews and swallows, eating with one hand and caressing my fingers with the other. I'm so... blown away by what he's saying. I mean, of course I always knew I loved him, but it used to be hidden beneath all these other things, like my guilt mostly. I suppose he had to hang onto something...

I just never knew my possessiveness and jealousy when it comes to Tate could be a positive thing for Ryan.

"Now, I'm not saying I want you punching him again." His face pivots in my direction as his grin widens. "Once was more than enough for that. But I just want you to know that I see your heart, Ben Lockwood-Harper. You wear it on your sleeve, and I'm smitten for it."

"Only for you," I bring his hand to my lips to kiss his knuckles. "And Jess."

"How many dudes have you punched for looking at her wrong?" He chuckles, and I have to laugh back.

"No comment." I attempt to smother my grin, but it doesn't really work.

Ryan devours his plate of food after that, and I honestly think it's mainly to make me happy, which has me soaring. Once he has food in his stomach, we grab a couple more drinks, though I know he's registering my wordless request for him to take it easy.

But it *is* a celebration, after all. And based on how much fun Ryan is obviously having, we might need to think about venturing into gay clubs on occasion. Because he clearly likes this, and while I'm not a partier, I want to make him happy more than anything else in the world.

I live for my husband and wife. Anything and everything I do is for them at this point.

Meandering around the party, however, is marginally irritating for me because I can tell all of Tate's friends know that he hooked up with Ryan. It's written on all their faces when we talk to them, and though the jealousy isn't a big deal, especially now that I know Ryan kind of likes it, the whole thing just makes me think maybe the hooking up wasn't as casual for Tate as it was for Ryan.

Ryan was sort of using Tate, to distract himself from what he wanted but couldn't have. It's a little fucked up, but then Tate has always been the guy who claims he doesn't have time for relationships. He revels in being single. If he were developing feelings for Ryan, I'm sure Ryan had no idea about it.

The sun sets, and on go the twinkly lights strung up over the backyard. It's actually gorgeous out here, and much more comfortable now that the sun has slipped away.

"Tell me you're at least having a little fun," Ryan hums, brushing his fingers through my hair while we stand off to the side, watching all the mingling happening around us.

I turn my face to his and give him a slow blink of appreciation, for how damn good his touch feels. "I'm having a ton of fun. Because I'm with you."

"Sweet," he smiles. Then the fingertips dance down my neck, tickling me just enough to give me chills.

My breathing shallows a bit as we stare at one another. Ryan's pupils dilate and he bites his lip.

I couldn't rip my hungry gaze away from his mouth if you paid me, and suddenly more than anything I'm feeling the heat in his hard body, so close to mine. The quixotic music rippling through the air, pushing us together.

I place my palm flat over his chest to feel his heartbeat and he leans in, kissing my lips softly, only once before trailing his mouth along my jaw.

"Can we *please* find somewhere to be alone right now?" He whispers and my cock throbs between us. "I've been dying for you all damn day and I can't take it anymore."

Swallowing, I whisper, "Take me wherever you want, baby. I'm yours."

He lets out a soft rumble of a sound, then immediately

grabs my hand and starts pulling me toward the house. I can only hope no one's paying attention to us, but honestly the way I'm needing this right now, I can't find it in myself to care.

We rush inside, passing guys left and right who are laughing and hanging on each other. We clearly aren't the only ones with this idea, and we're definitely not the only insatiable couple at the party. The first door Ryan tries opens to reveal three guys together in a bedroom, all of whom happen to be in *very* compromising positions. We both stand in that doorway for a few generous seconds before closing the door and turning away to try another room.

"Did that turn you on as much as it did me?" Ryan breathes while we stalk the hallway.

I can feel the flush in my face as I nod. *Never seen that happening in real life before... Damn.*

The only room that isn't locked or occupied ends up being a sun room, which wouldn't be a problem, except that it's made mostly of large bay windows which overlook the back patio... where the rest of the party is going on. It's sort of elevated, so it's not like people would be able to really see us unless we were fucking up against the glass, but still... The room isn't private by any means.

Not to mention there's no door to close. Anyone could just walk right in.

And for some reason, right now, that fact is turning me on more than I can even understand.

"We could always go into the bathroom if you want," Ryan suggests as we enter the sun room. "Or the closet."

"I'm not going back into the closet for anyone, baby," I grin at him and he laughs, draping his arms around my shoulders.

He hums while he kisses me slowly, softly, yet so full of passion I'm going out of my mind already. With his tongue in my mouth, his teeth nipping at my lips, I'm dizzy. I can barely stand up.

The sounds of us kissing and panting ring throughout the room. In all honestly, we sound like animals already and we just got fucking started. And it sort of ramps things up, too. We're becoming increasingly frantic, ripping at one another's clothes, eager fingers gliding across surfaces in anticipation.

The shirts come off. Then the pants are unbuttoned and unzipped. And I fall to my knees.

Biting my lip, I gaze up at my husband from the floor while he looks down at me, brushing his fingers through my hair with needy flames of green in his eyes.

"I want you," I tell him in a growl, breaking our stare to tug his pants down, just enough. I hear him hum when his dick is in my hand, then groan when I extend my tongue to lick his crown.

"I want your mouth," he whispers. "Your tongue... Your fucking throat."

He shivers when he gets what he wants.

I suck him between my lips, getting lost in a trance of blowing him with his hands on my head. I *love* being this for Ryan... Something for him to play with. I love how the dynamic between us shifts when we're getting physical. It always has and it's been the biggest turn-on of my entire existence.

"Baby, fuck me with that sweet mouth," he croons from above my head and I'm *dying*. I need to free my cock before it breaks off in these pants.

Rumbling with his solid flesh pushing down my throat, my jittering fingers pull my own dick out to stroke it hard in my fist.

"Oh I love that," he leans against something while gripping the back of my neck. "Look at that big cock..."

I pop off him to breathe, "Ryan, you're making me crazy."

I've got him in one fist and me in the other, catching my breath while watching his dick as if I expect it to do something.

"Sorry, babe. I'm so fuckin wound up right now," he lets out a breathless chuckle.

"Is it considered rude to fuck in a stranger's sun room?" I ask, peering up at him while my face heats beneath his salacious gaze.

"Would it matter?" He smirks.

I shake my head slowly as he hauls me up then pushes me back onto something. A couch? A chair? I would have no idea because I'm too busy focusing on my husband while he tears my shorts off and slides his hands up my hips.

"I wanna put my dick in you, Ben," he growls, coming over me to tease my lips with his, rubbing his erection on mine until they both flinch together. "*Deep.* Like, very fucking deep."

I can barely breathe, panting and purring and just fucking *needing* him with every ounce of myself. "Please... Please, *yes*."

"Please what?" He mumbles, kissing my neck, sucking hard until I'm sure there will be a mark.

"Fuck me," I insist. It comes out so damn needy, and I'm not even mad at it.

He rumbles into me while I touch him everywhere, tracing the lines of his chest, his abs, all that definition that makes him so masculine. The other part of my sexuality I never knew about until Ryan... That I want rough and rugged, too. Muscle and hair and a big dick.

It's still a little baffling, but I love the eager shivers it gives me when I look at him. When I feel him.

When he rips open a packet of lube with his teeth and squeezes it all over his fingers, swiping them between my ass cheeks.

"*God*..." I whimper at the sensation of him pushing into me, knuckle deep.

He pumps it for a moment, then adds another and I wrap my legs around him as much as I can because he can't go anywhere. I need him right here, like this, forever.

"You're so hot and tight, husband," he breathes as if he's astonished, awed, though we've been doing this for over a year.

I get it, though. I'm still amazed at how good this feels.

Ryan kisses my lips and I hold his jaw, kissing him back harder, devouring his mouth, tasting him, like cherry-lime from whatever he was drinking. It's delicious, almost as much as him pressing on my prostate until I turn to a puddle of need.

He pulls back, kneeling between my legs on whatever piece of furniture we're on, holding them apart wide as he massages the lubrication onto all his inches. I can't help but stare at his dick in all its glorious perfection. Long, thick, plump head, *veins* and stuff... Just, *God damn*. It's hypnotic.

An interesting scent brings my gaze back to his. "Did you use the banana lube?"

He pauses for a moment and glances at the empty packet next to us. "Uh, yup. Looks like I did."

"Lord," I can't help but laugh as he chuckles along.

He brushes my lips with his while rubbing his slick, banana-scented erection all over me. "You want this banana, baby?"

Now neither of us can stop laughing. But it does nothing to kill the mood. In fact, this is peak Ben and Ryan, right here. I'm having so much fun with him... *I always do.*

"I love you," I whisper, pulling his mouth back to mine to kiss him, leisurely while our heated flesh presses together. Writhing into one another, I reach between us and grab his dick, needing it inside me before I burst.

"I love you more than even seems possible, Ben Lockwood-

Harper," he tells me, causing my heart to thump aggressively behind my ribs.

"Fuck me, baby," I plead.

"Take my cock, Ben," he keeps kissing me, allowing me to press him up to my ass.

The smooth head of his dick nudges my hole and I tremble. Ryan's hands caress my hips, holding me hard while I push him inside, my body welcoming him with no more than a little effort.

"Fuck fuck fuck that's... *good*..." I groan, barely aware of what I'm saying as Ryan takes over, thrusting deeper. "Fuck *yes*, baby."

"That feel good, beautiful?" His hot breath dances over the flesh of my throat while he pumps, building up a rhythm with his hips, driving into me slow. At first.

"I love how you fuck me." Holding his neck, my fingers slink up into his hair, tugging him so he has to look at me.

Our eyes connect, his deep mossy green shining down on me while he moves between my legs. It's erotic, sensual and consuming... everything I've come to love from sex with my husband.

"You make me crazy, baby," he pants over my mouth, picking up the pace a bit, rippling into me, lancing my prostate until precum is pulsing from my dick. "The way your body holds onto me..."

"We fit together perfectly." My eyelids droop from the intense pleasure. The burn that feels amazingly good, like being set on fire with love.

"Mmm... your sweet ass swallows up my cock," he grunts, bottoming out then pulling back, enough to slam back in.

I groan out loud and he gives me a look. So I bite my lip to try and stay quiet, gripping fabric at my side while his thrusts pick up and he starts to really move. He's like an animal right now, a machine, his pelvis smacking against my ass while he fucks me deep and fucking *thorough*.

I know I won't last. I can feel the orgasm building already.

The piece of furniture is moving with us, the sounds echoing through the room. We're both sweating together, hot and slick and it's just adding to the feeling. The rough and deep I crave night and day from him... I can't get enough. I never will.

"I'll never get my fill of you," I tell him, voice hoarse and ragged in between him pounding me in the ass. "I fucking need this, Ryan. I need you."

"I'll always need you, Ben." He blinks at me, then drops a surprisingly gentle kiss on my lips.

His strong hands and fingers glide all over me, while mine hold him by his ass, keeping him deep in me, the pleasure raging through my loins like a storm. I'm going to come *soon*. There's no way I can hold off, and I have no desire to. The friction of his body brushing my erection is more than I can bear, in conjunction with his dick hitting my spot over and over again.

"I wanna watch you come from my cock in your ass," Ryan rasps, moving back to look down at me, hands gripping my pecs. His thumbs circle my nipples and my eyes roll back. "Let me see that big dick come, baby."

This is all too much. I'm wound up and about to snap.

"Ryan..." I gasp, my back arching. He holds me still beneath him, pushing and pushing and *pushing*, turning my entire body into a buzzing ball of energy until I finally fall. "I'm... *coming*."

"Come for me, baby," he utters breathlessly while I erupt.

And he watches, hands massaging my skin as cum jets from my cock, all over my abs and chest. I'm trying so hard to be quiet, but it's virtually impossible when it feels like I'm in a spaceship cruising the Milky Way. My dick is pulsing out streams of cum while I've officially become a giant orb of pure sensation.

"God, that was hot," Ryan croaks, sliding his fingers through the mess I made on myself before bringing them to his lips. He slips them into his mouth and sucks my cum off, keeping my good feels going on for much longer.

"Come in me," I plead, sounding spent while he keeps pounding my ass, the tightness I can feel in all his muscles giving away how close he is. "Please, Ryan. Come in me, baby."

"I'm... gonna... fill you... *up*." He kisses me, growling into my mouth.

And I can feel the moment he lets go. I *feel* his climax, orgasm pouring deep into me. It shouldn't feel so fucking good, but it does.

Euphoric.

"I'm coming so good for you, Ben," he cries, quietly, on my lips as we kiss through his release.

We're kissing the whole time, touching everywhere. Sucking one another's lips, feeling the heat and the pleasure, and the love flowing between us, rushing like rapids.

My hands grip his jaw, feeling him flex while he comes down from the high. And then he purrs to me, like a spent kitten who needs a nap.

I love this kid... I fucking love him so hard it's almost unbelievable.

"You're a wonder to me, baby," I confess, and he chuckles, dark brown hair falling in his eyes.

I brush it away for him and he grabs my hand, kissing it before holding it over his heart.

"Is this how it was always supposed to be?" He asks, eyes alit with fascination. "Me and you... With Jess and Ethan and our home, our family. I mean, for a while I wasn't sure..."

"How it could work," I finish his thought, and he nods. "I

think it works simply because it does. Because this *is* how it was always supposed to be. You came into our lives for a reason, Ryan. And you... you became my reason for everything else."

He does a little pout then drops his forehead to mine. I have to chuckle because we're being so corny right now, and I don't want to cry, but like... how could you not?

All this unexpected stuff that happened... It was all for a reason. *Our* reason.

It takes us a minute or two, but eventually we get up and attempt cleaning our mess. I'm afraid to go near the big window, half expecting to look out of it and see the entire party gawking up at me like they saw the whole thing.

But there's no way that's possible. The thing we were on was nowhere near close enough for anyone to see us.

"I think there's a bathroom around the corner," Ryan says, and I nod while we get dressed.

But a moan stops us in our tracks. Ryan's eyes widen at me, matching my own expression before he turns toward the doorway. I don't see anyone, and we both inch closer to the entrance of the room, following the sounds of muffled groans and... suction.

"There's someone out there!" Ryan whisper-shouts.

"Out where?"

He points. "Just around the corner. Do you think they were watching us?"

My face heats up at the idea. "It's definitely possible..."

Ryan slinks over to the doorway and I follow him. We peer out into the hall, just outside the room and Ryan's hand slaps over his mouth while I fight not to roll my eyes.

It's Tate. On his knees.

Sucking a guy's dick.

CHAPTER THREE
Ryan

Tate pulls off the guy's dick, looking like absolutely nothing is going on. He actually looks less startled right now than he did when we ran into him at the bar earlier.

The guy, on the other hand, is visibly mortified.

He's a tall one... Probably like six-four, at least. Taller than me and Ben. And he has light hair, blonder than Ben's, too. He looks very... *large*. Like he might not be American.

My money's on some kind of Norse god.

"Hey, guys," Tate murmurs, wiping his mouth with the back of his hand while the guy frantically tucks his dick away. "What's going on?"

"Nothing," Ben answers too fast.

I peek at him, and he's all flushed. He thinks they were watching us fuck. And knowing Tate, it's a strong possibility.

"This is... really embarrassing," the guy says, his face even redder than Ben's.

It's all a competition between these two, I think.

"Is it though?" Tate arches a brow at the guy, standing up slowly.

The looks they're giving one another are intense. There's something happening here, and I can't quite figure it out.

Instead, I decide to try and cut the tension with my default politeness. "Hi. I'm Ryan." I smile at the guy, extending my hand. He looks at it for a moment before I pull it back abruptly, remembering that it's covered in banana lube.

"Um... I'm Lance," the guy does an awkward little wave at me.

I gesture to Ben, "This is my husband—"

"Were you watching us?" Ben barks at Tate and I cringe.

Ben has a skill. He can make anything in the world seem like Tate Eckhart's fault. It's met well with Tate's skill in not giving a fuck while pushing Ben's buttons.

Tate leans into Lance's side, who still looks hella uncomfortable, his eyes staying on Ben. "If you didn't want anyone to watch, why'd you do it in the room with no door?" He smirks, and I witness Ben swallow.

Ignoring them both, I look back to Lance. "So how do you two know each other?"

"I, uh... I should actually be going," Lance runs fingers through his hair, turning to Tate to mutter a weakened, "I'm sorry. I can't..." Before staggering off.

I watch him disappear then peer at Tate with raised brows.

Tate rolls his eyes. "He's straight... *allegedly*."

"Oh." I'm not sure how to respond to that.

"Yea. I knew him... a long time ago," Tate's gaze stays in the direction Lance just left. "He showed up here after I ran into him earlier. And I thought maybe..." His voice trails before he shakes his head. "I don't know. I have no clue what I thought. It doesn't matter."

"You have a type, huh?" Ben grumbles, and I elbow him.

"Do you want to get a drink and talk?" I ask Tate. I can feel Ben glaring at the side of my face, but I ignore him. Tate needs a friend right now, and above anything else, we can be that. "It might help."

Tate continues to stare off into space for a moment before he brushes it off, brow furrowing. "No. It's okay, Harper. Thanks, but I think I'm just gonna go out."

"Go *out*?"

"Yea. It's Pride," he scoffs. "I'm not gonna spend it at someone's house all night." He tugs a pack of cigarettes out of his pocket, sticking one between his teeth.

Glancing at my shoes for a moment, I feel a little like a loser. I thought this was it, yet to my surprise, the night is still young. *What the hell happened to me? I used to know how to party. Now, I'm a dad and I barely even remember how to go out.*

Ben grabs my hand, startling me out of my little pity party.

"Can we come?" He asks Tate, peeking at me for a moment, a small curve happening on his lips, which are visibly puffy from all the kissing we were doing moments ago.

Tate lifts his brow at Ben. "Have you been to a gay club before, Lockwood... *Harper*?"

Ben rolls his eyes. "No, but what does that matter?" He shrugs, "I'd never been to a Pride parade before today. We'd like to come with you. I want to... dance."

He almost chokes on the word *dance*, like it's so foreign coming out of his mouth, his throat is trying to repel the letters. It makes me laugh.

"Babe, you really don't have to—"

"I'm well aware of what I *have* to do," he hums, grasping my jaw with his strong fingers. "I have to make my husband happy. That's my main concern at the moment."

I pout at him, pressing a slow kiss on his perfect lips, his perfect mouth and all the perfect things that come out of it. *He's a gift, this man.*

"It would *really* make me happy to watch you dance," I grin from beneath his kiss and he growls, pushing his hips into mine.

"Only if I get to do it with you," he breathes, raspy and deep.

"Try and stop me."

We pull apart at the recollection that Tate is right there, and of course he's staring at us like he has no idea what's happening. It's the tiniest bit awkward, since the last time I saw him was at his apartment on Christmas morning, after he let me fuck him knowing full-well I was madly in love with two other people.

We've managed to avoid each other since then, though we've heard through my brother-in-law that he's been doing great, apparently having become even more of a workaholic in the last year. He sent a gift when Ethan was born, and Jess made sure to send him a Christmas card at the holidays. But I think we all agreed maybe some time apart was best for the friendship.

It does suck, though. Because Tate was a true friend to me when I needed one. And sure, there was a sexual nature to it, which was hugely important to me coming out as bisexual. If it weren't for Tate, I may not have picked up on this side of myself right away. Or at least it would have been much more complicated for me to navigate.

As crazy as it sounds, Tate brought me back to Ben and Jess. For that, I'm eternally grateful. And I don't want him to feel bad, or to be upset about his love life issues. I'd like to try and help him the way he helped me.

Okay, not the same way. Just in a supportive, friendly capacity this time.

"So where we going?" I ask Tate and he says nothing, simply motions for us to follow him.

Here goes nothing.

THIS PLACE we find ourselves in is unlike anything I've experienced in my twenty-three years of life.

The building is huge inside. And spread out, like it should've been a warehouse. Or maybe it was one before. There are two bars across the space from one another, and a few scattered pieces of furniture here and there, but outside of that it's all open for dancing. And there are these stage-like boxes in the corners with stripper poles in the middle, complete with guys in thongs dancing on each.

I'm unable to tear my eyes from them for a moment because of how *naked* they are. There's nothing more than a thin piece of fabric separating their dicks from the world. It's... wild.

As we weave between all the hot, sweaty bodies grinding on each other, I notice that there are cocktail waiters wearing pretty much the same thing, walking around with trays of those little test tube shots. Tate grabs one while we slink past, sucking it down as the guy with a rainbow bowtie hanging around his neck forces a scowl. Tate simply winks at him and he grins back, which makes me think they might know each other.

In fact, I think Tate knows a few people here. He's being waved at left and right. I mean, I've always known Tate is popular. And his presence in this place is so very different from Ben and me, who are awkwardly clutching one another for dear life, completely out of our elements.

The place is *packed* with men. It's like a sea of muscle, overload for my eyes, most of them dancing close, making out, or singing along to the house-type remix of an Ariana Grande song. The air is muggy with sweat, cologne and masculine sexuality. It's an interesting vibe, one that I wouldn't mind being a part of from time to time.

Tate reaches a spot he deems fit for us to stop, by the bar, and props himself up against the edge. He grins and leans in closer so I can hear him shouting over the music, "Your eyes are so wide."

Ignoring my own insecurities, I tell him, "This is crazy."

"You want a drink?" He asks, eyes darting to the bartender —dressed only in tight leather shorts—who also seems to recognize Tate, a salaciously familiar smirk covering the rather beautiful man's lips while he holds up a finger as if to say *one minute*.

I look to my husband, who's gripping my hand so hard it's seconds from fracturing. Ben's eyes are all over the place as he takes in the scene, while simultaneously ignoring the couple dancing next to us, eyeing him like he's a bacon double cheeseburger at the end of a seven-day cleanse.

His blue gaze comes back to me and he pulls a grin, nodding, "Whatever you're having."

"We'll have two penis drinks." I turn to Tate and his brow quirks. "Do they do the penis drinks here?"

Tate laughs out loud. "You're so cute. It's Pride, I'm sure they can whip something up."

"Please stop letting him hit on you," Ben whispers in my ear, immediately giving me chills.

Tate is leaning over the bar to flirt with the bartender and order our drinks while I pull my husband close to me, playing with the hair at the back of his neck the way he likes.

"He's not hitting on me," I murmur, keeping my mouth by his ear so I don't have to yell. That and I want to give him chills right back.

"He is," Ben slides his hands down to my ass, gripping me hard enough that I gasp. "And you're not *his*, Ryan."

"Mmm... whose am I?" I trail his jaw with my lips, feeling him shiver in my arms, though he maintains his solid, growly Ben persona. Always in control... until his isn't.

I'm crazy for it.

"You're mine, baby." One strong hand glides up my back, holding me close to him while bringing his lips over my own. "You've always been mine."

"Always." The word barely makes it from my mouth before he kisses me.

It's so tender and full, I'm melting. His sweet, plush lips sucking at mine, warm tongue sliding in to taste me. I have to groan—I don't have a choice, it just comes out—my hips jolting forward to seek his.

And before I know it, we're moving together. We're kissing and *dancing*. Sort of...

Neither of us are big dancers, though I'm sure I've danced more than Ben has. I think he told me the last time he actually danced was on his and Jess's wedding day. Our wedding was more about moving between the bedsheets. No actual dancing happened that night.

But now here we are, in a club on Pride, hips swaying to the thumping bass of electronic beats, slow and gradual, building heat between us like a spreading fire. I think I recognize the song playing—it's Troye Sivan—and suddenly I can't stop my hands from running all over my husband.

You'd have no idea we just fucked not twenty-minutes ago from how much we're mauling each other right now.

Our kiss breaks so we can breathe, and I quickly glance at the bar to find Tate gone. There are two new elaborate rainbow drinks waiting for us, but I feel buzzed already and it has nothing to do with booze.

I'm drunk on Ben Lockwood-Harper, my gorgeous husband whose skin is warm beneath my touch; whose lips are soft on my neck, arms strong around my waist.

"Do you know how it feels to hold you like this?" He whispers on my flesh, just loud enough that I can hear him, the lust and love deep in his voice.

It reminds me of back then... How we fell in love so damn fast when we weren't supposed to. How he'd tell me things in a hushed voice that would linger in my head for hours and hours after he'd go.

"Yes," I answer him, chest to chest. Breathing, hearts beating together. "Because I'm holding you right back."

We move slow, easy, as his face pulls back so we can look at one another. His eyes are so blue, even in the darkness of the club. Surrounded by so much love, a pure celebration of it, Ben smiles at me. It's one of his subtle grins, though it shines like a beacon in the room.

"Thank you for being here with me," he hums then licks his lip.

I'm a bit hypnotized by it as I mumble, "I wouldn't dream of being anywhere else."

"I wish Jess was here too," he says quietly, reaching up to run his fingers through my hair. My eyes close for a moment.

"Me too."

"I think she'd love it." Then his index finger traces my bottom lip.

"We can bring her sometime," I tell him with wide eyes locked on his, wondering if he's *trying* to slowly seduce me with all these tempting touches.

Because if so, it's totally working.

"Or we can have a little after-party when we get back to the hotel," his brow cocks and I shiver at the sight. And the thought.

If there's one thing I can't get enough of, it's watching Ben fuck our wife. Or even more so, fucking him while he's fucking our wife. It's visceral, with us. A reflex, almost. Obviously, our connection runs so much deeper than just the physical, but there's no denying how mind-altering it is when we come together. *Pun intended.*

"That sounds like an excuse to leave early, my love," I grin, and he chuckles, caressing my throat with gentle fingertips.

"Let's stay just a little bit longer," he sighs. Now it's my eyebrow's turn to arch.

"Is Ben Lockwood having *fun* at a club?" I tease. "I'll have to alert the media."

"I just like spending time with my husband." He gives me a look. "Though the atmosphere in this place is pretty…"

"Hot?" I cut in and he smirks.

Looking to his left then his right, taking in the sight of guys all the fuck over each other, he peers back at me and nods.

I laugh. And then I kiss him.

And we dance.

It's a bit less of dancing than it is almost trying to fuck with our clothes on, though not so graphic. It's sensual, exotic. It's meaningful and it feels magnificent.

We end up drinking our penis drinks and ordering two more, both of us giggling at our purple tongues by the time they're gone. I really just love that we don't have to be anyone else here. Even if we didn't already feel inclined to be ourselves in day-to-day life, it's nice knowing we could come here and just *be*. We can be two men who dance and kiss and give each other the googly eyes without having to worry about getting looks. Without having to be on edge, wondering if it'll be a day when someone makes a comment.

I can't pretend it doesn't happen. Not often, which is amazing, and yet still sad that it happens at all. But here and now, we rule the world.

It makes me feel powerful, and happy.

It makes me fucking horny.

So when Ben slurs, "You ready to go, baby?" With his face tucked into the crook of my neck, I decide I need more of him right the hell now. I can't wait until we get back to the hotel.

I nod slowly and he straightens up, paying our bar tab and taking my hand. He walks us to the exit of the club, bidding our silent farewells to the party that's still raging even though it's after two in the morning. When we get outside, into the slightly cooled air of the late June evening, we start walking, past the rest of the crowd, who are making the sidewalk their own party spot.

We're only a ten-minute walk from the hotel, but as soon as I spot a dimly lit alleyway, I push Ben around its corner.

"Ryan, what are you—"

I stop his words with my lips, running my hands over the curves of his pectoral muscles through his shirt, feeling him up while I devour his delicious mouth and rub our crotches together. He seems startled, but only for a moment before he's giving in to me, grabbing my ass in two large handfuls.

"I'm so fucking lucky," I purr into his mouth. "I have the hottest wife, and the fucking *hottest* husband."

"I think I'm the lucky one," he rasps, our hardened dicks grinding together through our pants. The feeling is sublime.

"Call it a tie?" I breathe in between fierce kisses.

We're not far from the street, and it would be very easy for anyone walking by to watch what we're doing, but for the second time today, we don't seem to care who sees us. It's like part of the Pride experience... Fucking around for potential voyeurs. I'm totally fine with it.

"Benjamin," my voice comes out ragged as my fingers go

for the zipper on his shorts. It slides down while we pant together, eyes locked.

"Mmm..." his eyelids droop when I pull his cock out, stroking it in my fist.

Then I drop to my knees on the pavement and his eyes pop back open.

"Fuck my mouth," I plead with my gaze shimmering up at him, in between drooling over the sight of him, huge and hard right in front of my face.

He blinks. "What if someone sees?" His weak argument is met with a shrug of my shoulders while I lick warm lines up and down his shaft, savoring his *Ben* flavor, like clean flesh and hot man. "We could get arrested for this you know..." His fingers rake through my hair, gripping until I grunt.

"As long as you come down my throat, I don't really fucking care where we end the night."

I slide him deep into my mouth and he groans, my eyes popping up to his. He covers his mouth with his hand, and I think it's *beyond* sexy, that he can't be quiet with me.

I keep watching him, and him me while I suck, stuffing his girth between my lips, sheathing my teeth as best I can, tongue sliding. My head bobs and he pushes me, crown passing my gag reflex which I desperately try to ignore.

"*Fuck*, Ryan..." his head lolls back against the brick wall. "You suck me so good, baby." He grazes his fingers along my jaw. "You like having my cock in your mouth, don't you?"

I try to nod, already dizzy with lust, saliva collecting to fall from my lips. I swallow it, swallowing on Ben's dick, to which he releases a jagged sound.

"You've always wanted my cock in your mouth, huh?" He keeps running his dirty words, and it's driving me nuts. I have to rub myself over my pants because I need some relief. "Even when you weren't supposed to... you dreamt about sucking the cum out of me and swallowing every last drop. Didn't you?"

I groan around his dick, the truth in his words prompting me to suck and suck some more, until my jaw is numb and my brain is hazy. I reach for his balls with my free hand, caressing them the way I know he goes crazy for, and sure enough, he starts trembling above me. His hand is gripping the back of my neck, holding me in place while he flicks his hips, fucking my throat harder and deeper. It borders on rough, but I *love* it so damn much, frantically unzipping my shorts to tug my dick out so I can jerk off while I suck my husband dry.

I want him to come in my mouth. I want to make him come fucking gallons for me to swallow. I need it.

Come for me, Ben.

"Baby, yes..." His breathing is picking up, his moans turning frenzied, which I know means he's close. I just can't wait to fucking *drain* him. "You wanna drink my cum?"

His blue eyes burn down at me and I peer up at him beneath heavy lids, ready to collapse as I nod, mumbling on his cock.

"Yea, baby? You wanna swallow for me?"

Yes, I nod again. *Yes yes yes. Please, Ben.*

"Suck, baby. Suck suck *suck* out all this cum," he growls.

We both hear a gasp, eyes darting right to find two guys watching us, at the end of the alley.

They aren't close, not enough for me to really make out their features, but definitely close enough to tell that they're watching.

Ben's eyes meet mine once more, and together we silently agree that we don't care. It's actually... pretty fucking hot.

I'm beating my dick so fast, I'm about to erupt myself, slobbering on my husband's dick out in the goddamn open and not giving a single fuck who's watching.

The guys appear to be fooling around while they watch us, though I'm really not paying them any mind. I'm more concerned with getting my man off.

Ben's eyelids droop and he lets out a quiet rumbling groan. "God, baby, I'm fucking coming for you."

I'm so ready for it as his dick stiffens up to an almost insane degree before it begins pulsing, shooting bursts of cum into the back of my throat. I swallow it all, sucking him dry while he sings my praises above my head.

And then I come myself, aching throbs erupting from my dick, spraying my hand and the ground. And maybe Ben's shoes, who knows. But I really don't care.

The orgasm is freeing as fuck. I'm *high*, with my balls tingling and Ben's cock just resting in my mouth. His fingers brush through my hair, and I glance up at him, our eyes locked with so much love flowing between us. It's fascinating.

Pulling my mouth off him, I blink as he helps me stand on shaky legs. He licks the cum off my hand, then tucks my dick away before doing the same to his own, all while I'm just gazing at him and all his perfect features.

"You're so beautiful," I whisper, barely aware of what I'm saying.

Ben smiles, taking my face in his hands. "You're the most beautiful thing I never expected."

He kisses me, and I'm falling.

I'm *still* falling, more than a year later.

I'll never stop falling in love with Benjamin Lockwood.

CHAPTER FOUR
Jessica

My morning consisted of waking up to a crying infant. Ethan wasn't going crazy or anything, just letting me know he was hungry. And it wasn't until I had my boob in his mouth that I realized my husbands were still nowhere to be found.

I was nervous as hell, for all of five seconds before I carried our son into the living room of the hotel suite and found them both passed out on the floor. Pants undone, rainbow stickers all over their faces.

Ryan has giant, Jackie O sunglasses on and Ben's fingernails appear to have been painted.

My smile couldn't get bigger if someone stuck a clothes hanger in my mouth.

I decide to order breakfast before I wake them, calling down to the hotel restaurant for the works. Pancakes, waffles, eggs, bacon, toast, home fries... Literally everything. And three mimosas. Hair of the dog for them, and for me, well... I'm on vacation, dammit. *I pumped last night. I'll be fine.*

Once Ethan is done with his breakfast, I put him in his little playpen and decide to wake up the boys. It's clear from looking at them that they had an amazing night and I'm ecstatic for them. Sure, part of me wishes I could have been there. But the other part knows this was really important for them. Their first Pride ever being *out* and married. It's a huge deal.

There will be dozens more Prides in our marriage. I'll tag along next time, but this one was just for them. Plus, if we're being honest, I was in seventh heaven getting a solid night's sleep in that amazing hotel bed by myself. You have no idea how cramped it can get sleeping with two men every night. We upgraded to a California King and still I always have either Ben kicking me with his night-fidgets or Ryan burning me to death with his flaming-hot skin.

I did exactly what Ryan told me to do last night. After Ethan fell asleep, I ordered fried pickles and a quesadilla from room service and ate it watching reruns of *Bar Rescue*. Then I took a long, relaxing bubble bath in the massive Jacuzzi tub before knocking out into a deep, luxurious slumber, dreaming of my sexy husbands and all the delicious things they were most likely doing to each other.

It was a great night of *Jess time*. Much-needed.

And now I get to be present for the post-Pride hangover, which is really all I could ask for.

I kick Ben's foot a few times and he groans, before dropping to my knees to push Ryan's hair back with my fingers. "Hey... wake up, sleepyheads."

"Mmm..." Ryan's brow furrows and he tucks his face into Ben's back. "It's too bright in here."

"You're wearing sunglasses," I chuckle. "Big ones."

"What did we do last night?" He begins to sit up, rubbing Ben's shoulders, who's still in some awkward version of child's pose with half his ass hanging out of his pants. "After we left the club everything got fuzzy..."

"You dragged me to another party," Ben grumbles, finally straightening out and rolling over onto his back, rubbing his eyes hard with his hands. "With the guys who watched you blowing me."

I gasp, teasingly, and the two of them glance up at me, faking innocent looks. "So you two got into it last night then?"

"We didn't do anything too crazy," Ben says with sincerity lining his tone. He sits up and immediately rests his head on Ryan's shoulder. "But this one kept wanting to fool around in front of strangers."

"Um, I happen to recall the sun room at Tate's friend's house being mostly your idea."

"You guys saw Tate?" I ask, surprised, and also not, by this fact.

I keep up with Tate on social media, and it was never a secret that he'd be attending Pride in ABQ. But it's a big enough event that I figured we might not run into each other.

To be honest, I was sort of hoping we *would* cross paths. Tate is a good guy, a little misunderstood—mostly by Ben—but he means well, and I know he cares about Ryan. I've been craving a friendly reconciliation for a while now, because he's one of Jacob's—Ben's brother's—best friends and I'd like to invite him to family gatherings again. I don't want to leave him out just because he and Ryan... did what they did.

"We ran into him at a bar and he invited us to his friend's house for food," Ben says, noticing that my gaze is stuck on his nails. He holds his hands out in front of his face and his eyes widen. I laugh out loud. "When the hell did this happen??"

"I think that guy did it... What was his name?" Ryan's head cocks as he tries to remember through the obvious haze of alcohol still in his system. "Danny? Manny? Sammy?"

"Rico," Ben chuckles. "Yea, it was definitely him because he had acrylics and a full face on."

"He looked fierce," Ryan comments and Ben nods in agreement.

I have to laugh. They're so fucking cute like this. I'm more than a little obsessed with it.

Ben wraps his arms around my waist and pulls me onto his lap. "We missed you."

Ryan nestles up on my side. "How was Ethan?"

"Perfect, as usual," I tell him, dragging my nails along Ben's stubbled jaw. "So... how was Tate?"

Ben shrugs. "He's Tate. Always the same." Then he looks around me at Ryan. "What do you think the deal was with him and that guy?"

"The *straight* guy?" Ryan's brow cocks. "Who knows. They seemed to have some sort of tension happening. I hope they can make it work..."

"Tate doesn't want a relationship," Ben grumbles, playing with my hair. "He's a bachelor. I'm not sure he's ever even dated someone more than a couple times."

"Jake told me he was really into this guy he knew in college," I interject to share my knowledge on the subject. "*Lance* something."

Ben freezes and gapes at Ryan. "Lance... wasn't that the guy's name last night?"

Ryan nods. "Yea. Shit, you think that was him? Tate did say he knew him from a long time ago..."

I'm insanely intrigued by this. I remember when Jacob told me about Tate's college friend, Lance. Apparently, he was the only guy Tate's ever been in love with, though according to Jake, Tate would never use those words. But Lance had always been arrow-straight, so he sort of freaked out and vanished. And since then, Tate's been determined to prove how thoroughly uninterested he is in settling down.

I'm not one of those people who subscribes to the idea that

everyone needs to get married and have babies. Just because that's the life I lead, doesn't mean I'm going to say it's for everyone. Each person is different.

But I have to wonder if, at the very least, Tate might want to find someone to be serious with. I've gotten vibes from him before... And it makes my heart ache for him.

A knock at the door distracts us from the conversation about Tate's love life, and I jump up, scrambling to get it.

"What's that?" I hear Ben muttering, but as soon as I pull the door open, and the room service guy pushes in a massive cart covered in food, he and Ryan gasp out loud.

"Baby! You're the best!" Ryan mimics tears of joy, falling at my feet while I laugh, catching the room service guy chuckling, too. "I'm so hungry I could die."

"Well, no need to die, muffin," I drag him to his feet and deposit him next to Ben at the table. "Breakfast has arrived."

"And mimosas I see," Ben's grin is massive.

Once the hotel employee leaves, we all huddle together ready to stuff our faces with the most delicious looking and smelling breakfast of all time. Ben checks the monitor to make sure Ethan is still content, then we raise our flutes.

"I propose a toast. To the best first Pride ever," Ben sighs. "And the best husband and wife a guy could ask for."

"I second that." Ryan smiles as we clink our glasses.

"Cheers," I murmur with love in my eyes for these two wonderful men.

We sip our drinks and dig into the food, making nothing but yummy noises for a solid five minutes before anyone speaks again.

"I'm so glad you guys had fun last night," I tell them while pouring a bit too much syrup on my waffles. "The parade really was such a blast."

"It was amazing," Ryan nods. "I say we make this a tradition."

"I'm down for that," Ben agrees in between inhaling his food.

"And it's right around anniversary time," I bite my lip, eyes darting to Ryan for a moment.

"Is it?" He teases. "Hm. Guess I forgot."

We make faces at each other for a second, glancing at Ben who's too busy eating all the bacon to notice what we're saying. Ryan does a silent giggle of excitement and I kick him to make him stop before he blows our cover.

A few more bites and I'm full, so I go check on the baby. While I'm in there, making funny faces at Ethan that have him giggling up a storm, arms wrap around me from behind. Then kisses sprinkle along the nape of my neck and my shoulders, while I lean back into the young, hard body enveloping me.

"You smell tastier than the food," Ryan whispers on my skin, instantly giving me goosebumps. "Did you get that text from Jose?"

He said it quietly enough that I know Ben wouldn't be able to hear through the monitor, but I still pull him further away, nodding with my eyes widened in excitement. "It looks amazing!"

We both jump up and down together for a second, then stop abruptly, glancing at the doorway to make sure Ben's not watching.

"He said he's almost done," Ryan whispers. "I'm so excited for him to see it."

"Me too!"

We hear Ben coming closer, so we replace our sneakily eager faces with regular ones just as he enters the bedroom, making a beeline for the en suite.

Then he peers at us over his shoulder. "I'm gonna take a

shower." The look on his face is purely devious as he shoves his pants down, making himself naked before striding into the bathroom. Ryan and I share a look, both biting our lips before scrambling after him.

"I'll stay with the baby," Ryan tells me with a smack on the butt. "You go first."

Normally I'd offer to let him go first, but he had Ben all night and I'm in desperate need of some relief myself. So I drop a kiss on his lips and swing into the en suite, stripping and slinking into the shower with my husband.

Ben is a gorgeous man, we all know this. But Ben when he's naked beneath running water is unlike anything I could have ever dreamt up as a girl, fantasizing about my future husband. I also never could have anticipated having not one, but *two* delicious muscular husbands with massive dicks, so you know... Dream do come true.

Be jealous, it's okay. I know I'm a lucky bitch.

Ben runs his fingers through his wet hair, pushing the golden strands back before leaning up against the wall of the massive shower enclosure. "Hey, beautiful."

"Hi," I step beneath the water, letting it cascade over my body while my only focus remains on touching this perfect specimen of man. My fingers trace all the curves and sinews in his chest and abs while our eyes stay locked. "Missed you."

"Missed you more," he rumbles, holding my waist in his strong hands. "Here's what I'm gonna do, wife. I'm gonna wash you up, then I'm gonna make you dirty again." I chomp my lower lip. "Then I'm gonna send our husband in here to do the same thing. Sound good?"

A whimper breaks through while I nod.

His hand glides down to my ass and he cups it possessively. "I don't want you leaving this shower until you're overflowing with both of our cum, do you understand?"

"Yes," I mewl, grinding myself into him. "I understand."

"Good," he murmurs, and then takes my face and pulls me to him for a searing kiss.

It's not fast or hard, but slow and deep. Warm as hell and devouring, like he's taking his time because he can. That's Ben's signature kiss and it's deliciously overpowering.

Breaking for a moment, he grabs the soap and lathers it up in his hands. Then he proceeds to run them all over himself, then me, soaping us up good, before smooshing his hard body into mine, kissing me once more. *This is the most fun washing ever.* He slinks a hand between us, his thumb circling my clit while I purr into his mouth. My legs want to spread, but I'm standing so it's a little difficult. And yet Ben already has a plan.

He lifts me up without warning, pinning me against the wall of the shower while I wrap my legs around his waist. His warm mouth descends, sucking and nipping on my throat until I'm quivering. Then he positions us so that his erection is sliding over my slit and I moan at the sensation.

"Rub your wet pussy on my cock, baby," he growls, holding me in place while his mouth moves lower, onto my tits. I'm desperately writhing into him, dragging myself up and down all his inches as he sucks my nipple into his mouth, swirling his tongue around it.

"Fuck yes," I gasp, going out of my mind already.

"Sweet mother of God, that's hot," Ben rumbles with his mouth all over my tits, tasting and loving it, like the kinky sex god he is.

My fingernails dig into his shoulders as his movements become frantic and he reaches down, grabbing his cock in his fist and pressing it up to my tight entrance. I'm dripping wet already, so he has no issue sliding in. And we both groan in unison while he sinks deeper and deeper.

"You feel like heaven," his voice shakes as he rests his head in the crook of my neck, thrusting deeper still, until he's at the hilt. "This warm, tight pussy holding my dick..."

"God, Ben," I pant, gripping him between my thighs as he starts to move, fucking me against the wall.

"You love this big dick in you, baby?" He hums. And then we hear another groan.

My eyes open to find Ryan watching outside the shower stall, pants down just enough to have his dick in his hand.

Ben lets out a ragged chuckle while I watch Ryan watching me.

"I couldn't help it." His eyelids droop. "I *love* watching you two."

"I know the feeling," I gasp, scratching up Ben's back as he pumps into me, harder and harder.

I'm crazy for the feel of him inside me, especially at this angle, when his pelvis is brushing my clit.

"You want me to come deep inside our beautiful wife?" Ben turns his face just enough to peek at Ryan.

Ryan nods frantically.

Then Ben pulls back, still pinning me against the wall, holding me by my ass with one arm while his other hand goes for my clit. He rubs it softly, yet thorough—*a master of petting the pussy, this one*—while watching his cock move inside me, stroking my inner walls, pressing on my G-spot.

My head drops back against the wall and I bite my lip to keep the moans in. It barely works.

"Fuck me..." My hands move into his hair to pull it hard. "You fuck me so good, Ben."

"I love fucking you," he whispers, claiming my mouth, and that, paired with the sensations he's giving me below the wait, cause me to erupt.

My orgasm takes over, my body gripping him in contractions as I come hard all over him, crying his name into his mouth.

"That's it, wife," his voice is like the deep, seductive purr of a jungle cat. "Ride it out. Come hard for me, baby... Ride this cock."

I can't even. His dirty mouth is pure perfection.

Ryan is whimpering outside of the shower stall, and when my eyes finally reopen, I see him forcing himself to let go of his erection.

I have to chuckle sleepily. "You like that?"

"I swear to God, I could come just from watching you come," he rumbles.

"Ryan, come here," Ben demands, still driving into me, his movements picking up the pace.

Ryan steps out of his pants and enters the shower, immediately running his hands all over Ben's ass and hips while he thrusts into me over and over.

"Touch," Ben says in a plea, muscles tightening all over him, which tells me he's close.

Ryan runs his lips along Ben's shoulders, his fingers exploring where we're joined. Ryan touches Ben's dick while it moves in and out of me, circling my clit with his fingertips, rocking me with a whole mess of agonizingly beautiful aftershocks. Then with his other hand, he goes between Ben's parted thighs, massaging his balls and touching us from underneath.

"*Fuck*, baby..." Ben breathes, dropping his lips onto my tits once more.

"Jess, what do you think..." Ryan starts, mischief in his tone while he drags his fingers back between Ben's legs, "Would happen if I..."

I feel Ben stiffen, then shudder.

"Pushed inside our husband like this?" Ryan bites down on

Ben's shoulder and Ben lets out a jagged whimper, I'm assuming because Ryan just stuffed his finger inside Ben's ass.

"*Fuck fuck fuck*," Ben mumbles with my nipple between his lips, pounding into my pussy faster and faster.

"Mmmm..." Ryan looks at me over Ben's shoulder and winks. Then he does something that has Ben crying on my chest.

"I'm coming I'm coming... oh God... *yesss*..."

I can feel Ben's dick pulsing out his orgasm inside me and it turns me on more than I can even understand. Enough that I start coming again, just a bit. Just enough for me to go cross-eyed.

"Goddamn, I love you both," I gasp, hauling air into my lungs.

"Not done," Ben croaks as he comes down from his high. He lifts my hips a bit, then turns to Ryan. "Baby, I'm gonna pull out of our wife now. Don't let any of my cum escape her gorgeous body, got it?"

Ryan nods dutifully and I'm trembling in anticipation. I can't believe I just came a bunch of times because I'm more than ready to keep going.

Ben tugs himself out of me, sort of just handing me over to Ryan who, rather than stuffing his deliciously hard dick inside where Ben's just was, which would be amazing by the way, drops to his knees, draping my legs over his shoulders. He tucks his face in my pussy and licks and licks, tasting all of Ben's cum as it runs into his mouth.

I'm fucking *dying*.

"Jesus Christ," Ben gapes at him. "That's the hottest thing I've ever seen."

I can't stop panting while Ryan's eyes dart up at me, then over at Ben. The lust in his gaze is unparalleled while his tongue slinks inside me.

"I really don't want to leave this, but I have to," Ben says quietly, almost as if he's reminding himself as he rinses off. He places a soft kiss on my shivering lips then hops out of the shower to go watch the baby, leaving Ryan and me alone for our shower time.

And I'm winding up all over again.

Ryan's tongue is a *treasure*. It works literal magic on my clit and my lips as he sucks, nips and laps, around and around, through and through while my fingers twist in his dark, wet hair.

"I love your mouth on my pussy," I whimper, and he groans into me.

He makes me come two more times before he finally stops, letting out a rough breath as if he didn't want to pull away. But he does, standing up while placing me down on my feet. I wobble for a moment, unable to keep my eyes off his dick, which is rock solid and stretched, reaching out for me. I brush my fingers over it, and he hums. Then I go for his balls and he purrs, my eyes jumping back up to his.

The green is especially dark, like a forest of untamed desire as I fall to my knees in front of him.

He says nothing, simply stares down at me, and I up at him while I extend my tongue, curling it around the swollen head of his cock like a lollipop.

That gets him. His eyes droop shut, and he props himself up on the wall with his hand. So I do it again, this time sucking on his crown until I can feel him stiffening.

"*Fuck*, Jess..." His fingers twist in my hair, yanking enough to give me chills. "Suck me, baby."

Moving more of him into my mouth, I do just that. I suck on his solid flesh, bobbing for him, sliding him all the way back as far as he can go. I do this a few times before moving my mouth onto his balls, licking and sucking the way I know he likes it. It goes on for only a few minutes before he yanks me up and spins me around.

"Hold your ankles," he growls, bending me over.

I do as he says and before I know what's happening, he's pushing inside me from behind, filling me all the damn way up.

"God, that's... *good*..." He grips my ass hard in his hands while he fucks me, rough and deep and *oh so good*.

I'm going out of my mind, building to the brink once more. I reach out to hold onto the wall while his hips smack into my ass, *slap* and *slap* and *slap*. The friction of his thick cock inside me spreads a wildfire of need through my body. Ryan holds me close to him, bringing a hand around to rub my clit while he fucks me, sucking and biting my neck.

"Will you come with me, baby?" His voice vibrates into me, all but snapping with his obvious need to come.

I nod fast. "Yes. Yes yes yes, I need to come with you, Ryan."

"I love you, Jessica..." he groans, pushing and pulling and pushing until, "I'm... fucking... coming... in... you."

We're a symphony of squeals and groans as he erupts into a staggering orgasm, throbbing into me as I break at the feeling, throbbing around him. My pussy swallows up his cum, mixing it up with Ben's, the thoughts of which has me soaring for far longer than I could have imagined was possible.

"Wow..." We hear a deep voice and both of us turn, spent and practically falling over, to find Ben watching us with wide eyes, thumb running over his lower lip.

"How long have you been there?" Ryan breathes, pulling out of me and helping me get re-cleaned up

"I love seeing you two come together," Ben grins. "Hottest thing ever."

Ryan bites his lip, soaping up my tits while I giggle, doing the same to his dick.

"Okay, actually *this* might be the hottest thing ever," Ben grumbles, rubbing his jaw before turning away. "I need to leave before I get sucked back into that shower."

Ryan and I just laugh out loud.

HOURS LATER, we've finished having dinner at a lovely Italian place with outdoor seating, and now we're taking a walk through the park with Ethan in his stroller.

It's been a perfectly beautiful day. I couldn't have asked for a better long weekend.

Ben picks Ethan up out of the stroller and starts swinging him around while Ryan and I laugh.

Ryan's wiping his eyes, sighing out his chuckles as he says, "That girl over there looks exactly like Hailey."

I'm finishing up my own giggles as I turn in the direction he's looking, the smile sort of simmering on his face. "Where?"

He nods, squinting a bit. "The blonde over there, making out with that dude."

Of course I see the couple he's referring to, but I've been pretending not to notice them, since they're all over each other and seemingly unaware that this is a public park. But now that I'm looking, my stomach is getting all twisty. And my chest is tight.

"Oh Jesus..." I mutter, feeling Ryan stiffen at my side.

We share a look, eyes wide, conveying the same thought. *That is Hailey. And Ben's going to lose his shit if he sees what she's doing over there.*

Our eyes dart to Ben who's in his own little world, tickling Ethan, smiling and being just the hottest damn dad on the face of the earth. I really don't want him to freak out. And not that he even should. I mean, Hailey's a grown-up, and we're married to her ex.

There's a certain level of shit she's going to get away with for the rest of her life. *She kinda has us by the balls.*

But even so, even after everything that happened, Ben still manages to be overprotective of her, though he has loosened the reins quite a bit in the last year. She lives here in ABQ, in her own apartment off campus. She does her own thing, but still comes to visit once a month for dinner. I think Ben will always see her as his little girl. That said, he's also had his hands full over the last eighteen months, and hasn't had as much time to dedicate to worrying about her.

Still, I witness it; the moment he notices the couple making out on the park bench not thirty feet from us. The moment he notices that the girl in this equation is his *daughter*. And ultimately the moment when he goes into rage-shock.

He blinks a few times in their direction and time actually stands still. Ryan is squeezing my hand to death, which doesn't make me feel good at all. It just means he knows our husband's about to explode and there's really nothing we can do.

Ben places Ethan carefully back into his stroller, buckling him up and giving him his pacifier. And then he's off, stomping in the direction of our twenty-year-old daughter and the guy whose face is still attached to hers.

Ryan grabs the stroller and we power walk behind Ben, trying to intercept.

"Babe," I call to him, grabbing his arm. "Please..."

"Please what?" He growls, quietly, turning to face us. "Do you see this? She said she was going away for the weekend!"

I flinch. Because yea... she did say that.

"It's Monday," I shrug, defending our daughter. "Maybe she just got back."

Ben rushes out a sturdy breath, shaking his head as he

continues on marching. The four of us stop right in front of the bench, and I'm trying desperately to project some motherly telepathic advice to my daughter who hasn't come up for air in minutes at this point.

Uh, Earth to Hailey! Stop frenching the dude and pay attention! Your dad's about to blow a gasket.

Hailey finally, *finally* pulls off the dude who, now that we're closer, is visibly older than my daughter, and turns her face to glare at us as if we're random strangers who are suddenly too close to her make-out party.

But when she realizes it's us, her face goes ashen. Seriously, I've never seen her pale so fast.

"Dad," she gulps, then glances to me. "Mom.... Ryan."

Ryan does a cute little wave, always trying to be more of a friend to Hailey than anything. It's still difficult, after all.

Hailey accepted our relationship, the marriage and everything. She's been supportive, but then we also only see her once a month. It's a bit *out of sight, out of mind* for her, which is totally understandable. But when we do all spend time together, Ryan acts like Hailey's friend more than he acts like our husband. We purposely refrain from any displays of affection because we don't want to make her uncomfortable.

Of course she gets it, but it's a work in progress.

"Who's this?" Ben barks, and Hailey jumps.

"This is... Oliver," she answers calmly, though I can tell she's nervous as she glances to the grown-ass man at her side. "Ol, this is my dad, Ben, my mom, Jess, and my..." She pauses, gaping at Ryan while he rubs the back of his neck, like he's in physical pain from the awkwardness of the situation. "This is Ryan," she sighs, exhausted already.

The guy quickly ditches his uncomfortable grimace and pulls a wide smile. "Lovely to meet you all." He has a British accent. *Interesting.* "And who's this little guy, then?" Oliver asks, leaning in to wave at Ethan.

"This is Ethan," Ryan smiles while Ethan the ham gobbles up the attention from the stranger.

"What a nugget," Oliver grins.

I can't help but swoon, just a little, to myself, because he's *gorgeous*, and that accent? *Yum.*

But then I'm reminded that my daughter was just sucking face with this guy, and he's clearly in his early thirties, *at least.*

"I thought you said you were going away for the weekend," Ben says to Hailey, and it becomes apparent in this moment that he's not mad about her making out with a guy as much as he is hurt that she didn't tell us she'd be around today.

Ben invited Hailey to tag along to the parade with us, and I think deep down he was feeling a little insecure that she said no. Of course she claimed it was because she already had plans, and Ryan and I were inclined to believe her. But Ben still harbors a lot of guilt with Hailey. He doesn't have to, but it's just the way he is. It'll take him a bit to get over it.

"I did. We just got back this afternoon," Hailey answers defensively, but then her eyes widen.

"*We?*" Ben's jaw clenches visibly. "As in... you two?"

"No," Hailey gasps. *Obviously lying.*

"It's very nice to meet you, Oliver," I hip-check Ben out of the way before he murders someone, extending my hand to the man. He gives me a polite smile and shakes it. "I apologize for my husband. Well, that one." I grin, nodding in Ben's direction. Oliver looks overwhelmed, but he forces himself not to react, which I have to appreciate. "So, how do you two know each other?"

The polite smile I was getting a second ago turns strained and nervous as he glances at Hailey. Then back to me. Then to Hailey. Then me.

What the hell is happening right now?

"What a minute," Ryan bursts into the conversation, after pretending to be invisible this whole time. *"Professor Morrison?"*

Both Ben's and my faces spring in Ryan's direction to find him gaping at Oliver like he recognizes him. Then we turn to Oliver, who looks like he's preparing to get up and run away at any moment.

Instead he lets out a strained puff of air. "Right. So you recognize me, then."

"I took your class freshman year," Ryan actually grins, like he's excited to see an old professor. Until he realizes Ben's glaring at him and forces the smile off his face.

Hailey takes a deep breath. "Look, I was going to tell you guys about this when it was more serious..."

"You mean, more serious than making out in a public park?" Ben hisses and Ryan places a hand on his shoulder in an attempt to calm him down.

Hailey ignores her father. "But yes, Oliver is... my teacher. He's a sociology professor at UNM."

My blinking suddenly becomes rapid. I don't really know what to think, feel or say in this situation. On the one hand, I can't be a hypocrite. I can't tell my daughter what to do, especially when she's an adult and fully capable of making her own decisions. But then... I'm also her mother. And she's dating her professor, which isn't my favorite. Not when we're paying thirty-thousand dollars a year for that school.

"I loved your class, by the way," Ryan mutters.

"Alright, that's enough," Ben seethes. "Hailey, how could you be dating your teacher? How old is he, anyway??"

I want to cover my face with my hands. This is too painful to watch.

Hailey folds her arms over her chest. "He's thirty-six. You got a problem with that, Dad?"

Ben opens his mouth, but then snaps it shut. He has not a single leg to stand on in this argument. Because that's almost *exactly* the same age difference between us and Ryan. And at least Oliver isn't Hailey's daughter's ex...

"No... no problem with the age." Ben swallows visibly, tightening his fist over and over at his side.

It's actually kind of funny to watch. He's being forced to heel, which is something Ben hates. I find it amusing. And sexy.

"The control freak is about to lose it," Ryan whispers in my ear and we both giggle.

Ben glares at us. "This isn't funny, you two. She's dating her professor. That's messed up!"

"Worse than marrying her ex...?" Oliver mumbles.

"Whoa, cheap shot," Ryan says, holding Ben's shirt to keep him in place, as he's clearly preparing to lunge. "Professor, we just want to know that you're not taking advantage of Hailey. She's a wonderful girl, and we'd hate to see her get hurt."

"Really, Ryan?" Hailey gives him a fiery look.

Ryan holds his hands up. "Okay, I'll see myself out."

"You guys, I'm fine," Hailey hisses then rolls her eyes. "I know what I'm doing, and you all need to stop treating me like a kid. Oliver and I are dating. We have been for a couple months, and the only thing you need to know is that I'm safe and happy."

Now it's Ben's and my turn to share a look. She's right, though. We've always been a bit overprotective of Hailey. But maybe it took everything that happened with Ryan for us to finally cut the damn cord, so to speak.

"We're happy you're happy, Hailey bug," I tell her, leaning in to give her a kiss on the head. "And we're even happier to see you. I think that's why your dad is wound up. It didn't feel right coming to ABQ and not meeting up."

Hailey lets a smile out, peeking up at Ben. "I know. It's great to see you guys, too. I really want to hear all about your day yesterday."

Ben sighs and reaches out to take Hailey's hand in his. "I can't wait to tell you about it, baby girl. Why don't you come home this weekend? We can have dinner... We miss you."

Hailey looks between me and her father. We're both sort of pouting, which makes her laugh. It's only been three weeks since she last came home, but still. Finding out she's dating someone... her professor, no less... I think she owes us another visit.

"Alright, that sounds fun," she sighs. "I'll come down Saturday."

"Yay," Ryan cheers quietly and Hailey laughs.

"Yea, I mean, how can I miss the big one-year anniversary, right?" Her head tilts. "Are you guys having a party?"

I glance at Ben. *She remembers our new anniversary with Ryan? Is that weird?*

I have no clue anymore.

"We were gonna keep it casual," Ben says. "But now that you're coming, we can do a little barbecue."

"Sounds great," Hailey smiles.

I give her another kiss on the cheek, as does Ryan, then Ben. Ryan and I turn to walk away, but Ben stays planted right where he is, watching the two of them expectantly until Hailey sighs and gets up, taking Oliver by the hand and dragging him to leave, waving at us as they walk away.

I can't help but giggle at Ben.

"Don't say a word," he grumbles.

Ryan and I look at each other and burst out laughing.

We don't even have to.

CHAPTER FIVE
Ben

"I mean... it's crazy right?"

"It's not *crazy*."

"Oh, it's crazy."

I'm pacing and I can't help it. This feels weird.

"Ben, you know no one appreciates your delusions more than me," Ryan says with an audible grin, though I'm not looking at him. I'm too busy prancing around the living room in a haze of worry for my only daughter. "But the way you're reacting to your daughter dating an older man is entirely hypocritical."

That gets me to stop. I turn my face is his direction, gaping down at him where he sits on the couch, eating an apple. As if nothing's wrong. As if my baby girl isn't being defiled by a predator nearly twice her age.

I shake my head a little. "It's not about the age. The age is irrelevant."

He lifts his brow, "Right," motioning a hand between the two of us.

I roll my eyes. *Yes*, Ryan is fifteen years younger than me, almost the exact same age difference between Hailey and Oliver Morrison. *Stupid British name, but whatever.*

But that's not the point.

"It's about him being her teacher," I grunt, giving my husband a warning look. "He's in a position of power and he used that to prey on her like some sicko. He's basically Harvey Weinstein!"

Ryan chokes on his apple and starts coughing, covering his mouth to mask the laughter. It makes me smile, but I'm desperately trying to cover it up as I take a seat next to him, rubbing his back. Once his windpipe is cleared, he turns to blink at me with amusement dancing in his evergreen green eyes.

"Oh, Benjamin," he sighs, reaching out to brush my hair back with his fingers, before trailing them along my jaw. "You're too pretty to have this many issues."

"You're not helping," I growl. "You're my husband, you're supposed to support me, no matter how ridiculous I am." I give him a pointed look, then take a bite of his apple.

"I'm just saying, she's an adult," he goes on. "You can't make her decisions for her, and you can't stifle her either. It's not like she's fifteen. Plus..." His voice sort of dissolves and he breaks eye contact, biting his lip.

"Plus what?" I narrow my gaze at him.

His eyes slide back up to mine slowly and he whispers, "He's like... really fucking hot."

I gawk at him for a solid three seconds before a laugh bursts from between my lips. "You're so annoying." He chuckles while I crawl over him, trapping him beneath me on the couch. "Is he hotter than me?"

"*Nobody's* hotter than you," he grins. And my lips brush over his.

"Only you," I press my hips into his until he hums. "Sexy ass husband."

"I love you," he mumbles as I kiss his soft lips. "And all your irrational, control-freakish ways."

Grinning on his mouth, I murmur, "I love you for loving me like this. You're perfect, you know that?"

He slides his hand up my chest. "Yea right."

"No, I'm serious. You are. You're pure perfection, Ryan Harper-Lockwood. I'm beyond lucky."

"Shut up or I'm going to pull you onto my dick right now," he growls through a smirk and I chuckle.

"What's stopping you?" I kiss his jaw, down to his pulse.

When he doesn't respond, I peek up at him to find him biting his lip, some sort of excitement he's barely able to contain radiating from his gorgeous face. My brows zip together in confusion.

At that moment, Jess waltzes into the room, making almost exactly the same face as Ryan. She nods at him, and he back at her.

I sit up slowly. "What's going on?"

"Ethan's down for his nap," Jess mumbles, practically vibrating where she stands.

"Let's go out to the shed," Ryan starts pushing on my chest until I climb off him.

"Why?"

"Could be fun," Jess shrugs. "We haven't hung out there in a while."

Ryan gets up, holding out the hand that isn't holding an apple for me to take, which I do, though still skeptical as hell.

"What about Ethan?" I ask while Ryan tugs me along, following Jess through the house, toward the back.

"He's sleeping," Jess says, opening the door in the kitchen

that leads to the deck. "I'm bringing the monitor. We won't be long."

Ryan tosses his apple in the trash, practically pushing me along, out onto the deck. We descend the stairs to the backyard, wandering past our rose bushes, and the lemon tree that's still going strong, toward my shed. Also known as the *ultimate man-cave*. More than even the basement, this place is still my special haven, though there's now an area of the room for Ethan's playpen and a few toys.

We don't have the same freedom we had for the last few years anymore. Now that Ethan's here, we have to be *on* constantly, which is when having two partners comes in handy. We agreed when Ethan was born that we'd work as a unit with him, and make everything even amongst the three of us. So if Jess and I need some alone time, Ryan will watch the baby, or if they need alone time, I'll do it. The only time it gets a little complicated is when we all want alone time together, the three of us.

But there are no shortage of people willing to babysit, between Marie, Jess's sister, her best friend Rachel, or Laura, my sister-in-law. The ladies have got us, which is much appreciated. Ethan's still young, but he's also a really low-maintenance baby. Life has changed, but we adapt.

Apparently, we're good at it.

We get to the shed, but Jess doesn't go to the door. Instead, she walks around the back. And immediately I notice something is different.

There's a stone path. *That's new...*

"Where'd this come from?" I ask, but they both ignore me, dragging me around to the other side of the shed, which is sort of secluded, between our property line and a bunch of trees. I've always wanted to do something back here, but I couldn't decide exactly what.

As soon as we're on the far side, my eyes widen, damn near bugging out of my head.

There are lights strung up in the tree branches, and a full stone patio with an elaborate hot tub built into the middle.

The thing is *amazing*. I've never seen anything like it. The hot tub's not huge, but clearly big enough to fit three people comfortably, which is all we need. It's lit up inside, shining blue light which isn't that visible since the sun's still out. But I imagine this will look *insane* at night.

There are plants and shrubberies set up to surround the edges of the patio, which serve as a barrier of sorts, for some privacy I'm guessing. As we walk closer, I notice how intricate all these details are… Cup holders for drinks, little fire enclosures, probably for when it gets cold. And the stonework is beautiful.

I'm stunned. *How in the hell???*

Finally tearing my eyes from the hot tub, I glance at my husband and wife, who are clutching onto each other, wearing massive, elated smiles as they stare at me in suspense.

"You guys did this…?" My voice comes out soft and hesitant because… *wow*. I'm blown away.

They nod frantically and whisper, "Happy anniversary."

I blink, stunned. "For me?"

Stepping up to them, their hands come to rest on my lower back, the three of us huddling together a bit. I'm just gazing at them in awe, speechless and perplexed that they'd do this for me.

"The traditional first year anniversary gift is paper," Jess says. "But paper is boring."

"Yea, and we're not traditional," Ryan adds.

"I can't believe you did this," I breathe, turning over my shoulder once more to look at the setup. It's beautiful, exotic, secluded. *Perfect* for the three of us. "When did you do this? How??"

They both laugh. "We had some guys come in last week and prep the area while you were at work. Then they did the patio and installed the hot tub over the weekend."

"So while we were at Pride, you had guys over here working on this?" I grin. "You're crazy. That's... awesome."

"You love it?" Jess squeals, and I nod.

"Yes. Yes yes oh my God, this is so cool," I chuckle, pulling her face to mine, kissing her lips slowly. Then I turn and do the same to Ryan. "I love you two so damn much."

"We love you too," Ryan mumbles on my mouth.

"I can't wait to play in here with you," I tell them.

Jess makes a little mewl sound and Ryan shivers. I can already tell this was the point... Something sexy for us to use together.

"We'll have to wait until this weekend to use it together," Jess says. "I can have Rachel come over to watch Ethan. Or maybe Hailey will do it when she's here."

I nod, keeping myself quiet. Little do they know, I have my own anniversary surprise for the two of them. And it'll definitely ensure some grown-up time alone.

I love my son more than anything in this world, but I'm gonna need at least a couple baby-free hours with my spouses in this sexy hot tub.

Grabbing both of them, one hand on each of their faces, I pull them to me and the three of us kiss together. I love doing it, because as uncoordinated as it is, it's *us*. The trifecta.

Ben, Ryan, and Jessica forever.

Jess whimpers and my dick stiffens. I would love nothing more than to keep this going, but I don't like leaving Ethan alone so far away, baby monitor or not. So we manage to pull off each other and go back to the house, waving bye bye for now to my anniversary gift.

It's okay, new friend. We'll be back.

IT'S LATE. Almost two in the morning. And surprise surprise... I can't sleep.

Insomnia is something I've been dealing with for a long time. Honestly, I think it started when my parents died. After that, I was always afraid something bad would happen if I fell asleep. Like someone I loved would be in trouble and need my help, and I'd be sleeping through it. It's an irrational fear, but one that definitely seemed to surface after the accident that took my parents.

And ever since, I've had trouble sleeping.

When you have a newborn, it's not too bad. I was all too happy to tend to Ethan and let my husband and wife sleep. But he's been sleeping through the night for a couple months now, and I continue my restless nightly routine.

Slinking out of the bed, I go downstairs to the kitchen to get some water. And then I contemplate going down to the basement to watch TV or something. But instead, I go outside.

To the shed.

Inside, I rummage around, making my way to the back-door. It leads right out to my new patio, which makes me smile.

They really thought of everything.

Wandering through the door, I turn on the overhead twinkly lights, bringing a dulled glow that gives it this almost mystical forest ambiance. Like I've been transported out of the Southwest and deposited deep in the woods somewhere.

Checking out the plants and flowers, I feel such a severe love for my husband and wife, in my bones.

The fact that I have people in my life who would do something like this for me... People who love me so much and so hard that they care enough to surprise me with something so special... It's thrilling.

"*Wow,*" I hear the word in a deep, smooth voice I've come to love listening to so much, sometimes I hear it in my dreams. My eyes lift to find Ryan gazing at me. "You are so fucking beautiful."

My lips curve a bit before I take him in, wearing only sweatpants pants, same as me, displaying all the definition in his torso, cut up muscles and lines everywhere. He's mouthwatering.

Not to mention the couple days of stubble lining his angled jaw, messy bedhead of chocolate brown hair flopping over his forehead. He's visibly younger than me... Not by much, but it's obvious he's in his early twenties. And I'm in my late thirties... which is why I can't say shit about Hailey dating an older man.

At the same time, I can. Because if that British dude is thinking anywhere near the sorts of thoughts about my daughter that I'm having about Ryan right now, I'd really have no choice but to murder him.

Ryan strolls over to me, not stopping until he's wrapped around me like a vine, pressing our warm flesh together, hands on my back, then my shoulders then my chest. Like he can't decide where he wants to touch me, sampling all the different spots.

"Did you get up to come find me, baby?" I whisper, taking his jaw in my hands and locking our eyes.

He nods. "I woke up... wanting you." I watch his Adam's apple slide in his throat. I want to bite it. "*Needing* you... I don't know why, but I'm craving it, Ben. I think I had a dream..."

"A dream that I was filling you up?" I whisper over his lips and he groans. "You're craving my cock deep inside you... right, gorgeous?"

He nods again, quicker this time. He's panting already and it's such a damn turn-on.

It's no secret that I like to bottom. It was the revelation of a lifetime when Ryan and I started hooking up, and it's definitely our default preference. But every now and again he'll come to me almost begging... Pleading for me to fuck him. And when he does, he wants it rough.

I can't say I don't understand his needs, because I most certainly do. It's something you'd never understand unless you experience it for yourself.

Ryan's basically ready to fall on all fours, which has me grinning. I *love* when he gets like this, and I love that I'm the only person who can give him what he needs in this moment. It's a power unlike any other, sating my ever-present need for control.

"We should really wait for Jess," I tell him while he spins in my arms, pressing his ass back into my growing erection. "You know she loves to watch you take my cock."

He's trembling, grabbing my hand and shoving it down the front of his pants. "I have an idea."

He pulls his phone out of his pocket, turning his face to smirk at me.

"You're wicked, kid," I tug his mouth to mine, kissing him hard, sucking his lips and biting him until he flinches, his cock doing the same in my palm. I cup his balls and he groans in my mouth.

"I desperately need a video of you fucking me," he breathes. "I've always wanted to watch it... To see how it looks."

"Oh, it looks fucking fantastic, baby," I tell him, walking us back toward the shed. "Let's go inside for this. I want my first time in the hot tub to be with both of you."

"Agreed." He keeps my hand on his balls and his ass on my crotch while we kiss our way inside and move to the couch.

We don't make it onto the couch, but rather on the rug in front of it. I shove Ryan down onto the floor, pulling his hips back so I have his ass right in front of me. He's already panting, face down ass up for me, and it's fucking wonderful. I squirm out of my pants, then remove his slowly, taking his phone.

I begin recording and prop it up so it's getting us at the right angle, wasting no time caressing my husband. I run my eager hands all over his muscular back and his ass, firm and full. The perfect ass on a man, dips in the sides and everything.

Ryan works out a lot. He loves it, actually. Sometimes we work out together, but it usually always ends up with us swapping sweat and DNA so if I want to take my workout seriously, I can't be near him. But he converted half the garage into his own little home gym, and I must say, it's really fun to watch him sometimes. All the flexing, the rippling muscles shimmering with sweat...

He's the *perfect* piece of man to quench my thirst.

My lips trail his spine, reaching his ass and biting him until he whines.

"Fuck you," he breathes through a laugh, and I chuckle.

"Mmm... is that how you wanna play it tonight, kid?" I kiss his smooth skin, dragging my lips closer to the crack of his ass, spreading him open with my hands.

"This is so wrong," he croons, turning his face until our eyes lock. "We're not supposed to be doing this..."

I let out an eager rumble. *Fuck yes, I love playing this game.*

"Relax," I rumble, pushing him forward forcefully, until his face is in the carpet. "No one will know."

He groans when my tongue feathers over his asshole,

stroking and swirling as he clenches like an instinct, before relaxing enough to let me stuff it inside. He whimpers and I hum because *Jesus Christ*, this is hot. This is *so fucking hot* already. I need to slow my roll, but like... *Fuck. I want more.*

My tongue assaults him for a few minutes while I grip him hard by the hips, holding him still as he tries to squirm. I push him down so he can get some friction on his balls, and he's immediately writhing into the floor, rubbing his big dick everywhere while I eat his ass.

"I love how hard this makes you," I mumble into him, reaching around to graze my fingers over his throbbing length. "You're so big, baby. Big, juicy, *delicious* cock."

I flip him over onto his back, pushing his thighs apart so I can wedge myself between them. Glancing up at his face, I almost expire from how goddamn good he looks. Cheeks all flushed, eyes desperately trying to stay open, lips shivering. He's a fucking masterpiece this kid.

Leaning up over him for a moment, I drop a kiss on his mouth, then trail him, leaving kisses along his throat, down to his chest where I suck on his nipples, *hard*, until he's squirming more, gripping the carpet in his fists. I suck all over his pecs, leaving little nips here and there as I work down his abs, his pelvis, reaching his huge dick.

My eyes lock on his while I slide the head into my mouth, sucking hard, enough that I can taste his flavor already. Salty yet somehow sweet. *My Ryan.*

His fingers twist in my hair while I take him deeper and deeper into my throat, our eyes on each other's the whole time. I rock my hips against his leg, humping his thigh enough to get friction on my aching cock.

I suck his dick until my jaw goes numb, and spit runs from my mouth. I love it, though. I love tasting him, feeling how hard he is in my mouth. I love the sounds he makes, and how he pulls my hair. I love how he shivers when I move my mouth onto his balls.

"Does this feel wrong, Ryan?" My voice is hoarse with need while I gaze up at him, licking lines all over him.

"No," he gasps. "It feels amazing."

"This is our little secret, isn't it?"

"Yes..."

I pull back and flip him back over onto his stomach, pulling him so he's kneeling before me. Then I reach underneath the couch cushion for the lube we have stashed there, starting that first night, when we fucked in here. I can't believe it's been over a year since then... *When I took his butt virginity right there on that couch.*

And now he's my husband, and though it seems impossible, I want him even more.

Pouring some lube out onto my fingers, I stroke it on my cock before swiping them between his cheeks. He purrs and leans back against me, gripping my thighs while I press myself into his back.

"You're my treasure, Ryan." I kiss the nape of his neck, sliding my slick fingers over his hole. "I'm keeping you. Forever."

"I've never felt the way I feel when I'm with you," he says quietly, his wide chest moving with his heavy breaths.

It almost feels like we're back in that night... Back then, before he was my husband.

When we were just two nervous men, practically strangers, wanting each other and not understanding it at all. But not giving a fuck because it just felt too damn good to ignore.

Unable to wait one more second, I press my left hand on his pelvis, keeping him close to me while my right takes my cock and nudges it up to his ass. I can't stop kissing him everywhere I can reach, his neck, shoulders, back.

Then I bite down on him, simultaneously pushing my cock inside his tight hole. He lets out a ragged breath, trying to slump forward, but I hold him in place, my chest melting into his back while we kneel on the floor, my cock burying deeper and deeper inside him.

"Jesus... *fuck*..." Ryan whimpers, his head dropping as he takes my dick, his body welcoming me, though he's so tight it's a fight to keep moving.

"Baby, you feel so good around me," I rasp with my forehead on his shoulder, hips driving in deeper still. "You're so tight, Ryan. Your ass is gripping my cock..."

"Your cock is *massive*," he mumbles, a moan slipping out when I shift, hitting his prostate. "Oh *God*, tear me apart with that big dick, baby."

My balls draw up at his words and the sexy fucking tone in his love drunk voice. And of course at the muscles in his body stroking my dick... *I'm not gonna make it.*

I hold his pecs from behind while I mash my hips into his, getting all the way inside him and staying still for a moment. Ryan is writhing against me, grinding his ass to try and get me to move. It actually feels divine...

"Ride me, baby," I whisper in his ear, sucking the lobe and nipping it with my teeth.

He immediately does as I say, lifting his ass and then pressing back down, fucking me while I'm fucking him. It's incredible, and the sight is enough to have me on the brink already.

Which reminds me...

The camera. I'd completely forgotten that we're recording.

Reaching over, I pick it up, holding it at the perfect angle to get a POV shot of his ass moving up and down on my dick, stroking me so damn good I'm going out of my mind.

"That's it, baby," I tell him, his groans and pants picking up with the pace of him bouncing on me. "You like taking this dick deep?"

"Yes," he grunts, falling forward to hold himself up with his hands while he moves.

I can't resist bringing the camera underneath to capture the sight of his giant dick, hard as fuck bobbing around. There are so many amazing angles I'm capturing in this video... It's the hottest thing I've ever seen. This is better than any porn I've ever watched, and I'm fucking making it.

"You want it hard, love?" I growl, taking over and grabbing him by the waist, slamming my cock in him to the hilt. He groans out loud. "Like this?"

"Yes yes yes, *Ben*," his voice is fading as his back arches. "You fuck me so good."

"You like it rough and deep, baby?" My pelvis smacks against his ass, taking him for a ride. And he's loving it. *Fuck, so am I.*

"*Yes.*"

"Yes what?" I growl, digging my fingers into his flesh while I pound into him.

"Yes... Daddy."

I pause for a moment, the word ringing through my head on repeat. The way he said it, deep and raspy and overflowing with lust...

He's never said that before, but my dick seems to like it. In fact, my balls are tight and ready to explode.

Yes, Daddy.

I've never found that hot before... I always thought it was maybe a little weird. But from Ryan, right now... It's going to get me the fuck off.

"Say it again," I murmur, picking back up stroking my dick *deep deep deep* in him.

"Fuck me, Daddy," he whispers, and I groan. "Harder, *Daddy*."

"Jesus..." I'm wound up and about to snap. I put the phone down by our sides, making sure it can still get us in the frame. Then I pull him up again so I can hold his throat. "You're gonna make me come, baby."

"Come in me," he pleads. My eyes lock on his dick, eyeing the precum dripping from the head.

He reaches for it, but I grab his hand. "I want you to come just like this."

He nods fast. "I'm going to... If you keep hitting that spot."

I shift my hips and he lets out a strangled moan. "This spot?"

"Yes, Daddy." His lips curve a bit, head dropping back, giving me access to his neck.

"You're such a sweet, forbidden thing," I suck on his neck and throat, biting all over, leaving marks, and I don't care. "You want me to come deep inside you?"

"Please," he whimpers, breathing so unsteadily it's as if he can't get air into his lungs fast enough. My eyes are still on his dick, watching it move while I move in him. "Come in my ass, Ben."

My strokes are becoming frenzied while I push and pull and push. Until I snap.

My balls throb and I come like a fucking firehose, pouring inside him while I gasp on his sticky skin. "I'm coming, baby. Fuck, I'm coming so good for you."

"Shit shit shit..." Ryan mumbles, both of our eyes stuck on his cock while he erupts, shooting his orgasm all over the place. "Fuck, *Daddy*, that's so good."

"I love you," I hum as my hips slow, touching him everywhere, gripping his chest, kissing his neck, breathing him in and exhaling for him.

It's all for him. Everything.

"I'm so fucking in love with you," he croaks, hands gripping mine, lacing our fingers together.

We stay like this for a few moments, recovering, until we remember the camera again, turning our faces toward it.

"That was crazy," Ryan chuckles breathlessly, picking up the phone to stop recording.

"Mmm... crazy good." I pull out of him, slowly, then watch as my orgasm starts to drip.

"Crazy fanfuckingtastic," Ryan grins, biting his lip while fidgeting, his face all red and blushed.

I get up and grab a towel, handing it to him so he clean up a bit. I'm watching him closely, unable to stop. He's a true wonder, this kid. Our chemistry knows no bounds.

"What?" He asks when he realizes I'm staring at him.

I tug my lip between my teeth. "Nothing... just... the *Daddy* thing." He laughs and covers his face with his hands. I kneel down next to him, pulling his hands away. "It was fucking hot."

"Yea... it sorta just came out of nowhere." He blinks up at my face.

"Well, feel free to let it out again..." I lean in, "If the mood strikes."

He chuckles and grabs my face, pulling my lips to his.

We kiss for more minutes than I can count before we go back to the house. And I fall into a deep, satisfying sleep.

CHAPTER SIX
Ryan

My eyes are wide as I gaze upon the screen of my laptop.

I can't believe what I'm seeing. This is... exhilarating.

It's bad, and I just *know* I'll get in trouble if someone finds out, but *oh my God*, it's thrilling and I can't help that fact.

"You ready to go?" Jess's voice sneaks up behind me and I jump so high I almost hit the ceiling.

Slapping my laptop shut like the guiltiest person on Earth, I whip around in my seat to face her, trying to look as normal as possible while showing her a smile. "Yep."

She's too busy rooting around in her purse for the keys to Ben's truck to notice how crazy I'm acting, which is a very fucking good thing. I casually pick up my laptop and stuff it into a drawer I know no one will open, leaving the house with my wife, my heart beating out of my chest.

"You guys going?" Ben calls to us on our way out, and we turn to nod at him.

I need to go to a couple auto body shops to pick up parts I ordered for the Mustang, and Jess is tagging along. She's actually super interested in my rebuild, which is sweet since she knows next to nothing about cars. Sometimes Ben comes too, but he told us he had some work to do and had to hang back, even though it's Saturday and we both assured him he needs to relax. Naturally he wouldn't hear it.

Ben loves his job, and it's not out of the ordinary for him to work on weekends when it's needed, this time in particular since he took Monday and Tuesday off for Pride. However, tomorrow is our official one-year anniversary and we have reservations tonight for a quiet, romantic dinner. Though we all know the real party will start when the three of us get home, and will continue late into the night. Laura's babysitting Ethan until tomorrow afternoon, and we're finally going to christen the hot tub.

Basically, Ben needs to get all the work out of his system now because it's gonna be nothing but play for the next thirty-six hours. *Minimum.*

"Drive safe." He presses a sweet kiss on Jess's lips, then grasps my jaw, giving me one too. It's virtually impossible not to swoon with him, but I'm forced to keep it in my pants since we're on a mission. "Remember what I told you…"

I roll my eyes, though I can't help but grin at his control-freak ways. "Yes, Benjamin, I remember. Check everything before I accept it and don't let him talk me into more than I need."

He smiles and pats me on the ass. "Love you both."

"Love you!" We call out, already hopping down the front steps toward the driveway.

It's times like these when I'm grateful that Ben got a truck for work. We're picking up seats from one guy, and a custom steering wheel from another, and I'm not confident all these things would fit into the SUV which now belongs mainly to Jess and me.

The whole process takes several hours. Locating the proper parts for my baby—I named her *Veruca*—isn't always easy. It takes a lot of scouring through auto magazines, phone calls and haggling with dudes twice my age. That's why Ben is so insistent on me making sure they don't take advantage of me. Because I'm young and this is my first restoration, which apparently is like ringing the dinner bell for sleazy car guys with dollar signs in their eyes.

But I think I've done alright so far. Veruca is almost done. Her engine is totally rebuilt, the exterior looks sick, and now I'm just putting the finishing touches on the interior, with the seats and whatnot.

I've gotta say, it's really been so much fun doing this. Not only the process itself but also everything I've learned along the way. I think once I sell Veruca, I'll definitely use the money to buy another body and go for round two.

I feel like my dad would be proud.

On our way back home, I get a text from Ben:

Hubby: How'd it go?
Me: Great! Everything looks awesome and Bill took $100 off
Hubby: That's awesome baby! You're so good at everything.
Me: Shut up lol :-*
Hubby: Lol. So you guys on your way home?
Me: Yup. We'll see you in about 20 mins
Hubby: Perfect. Miss you.

I grin and shake my head, "He's fucking adorable."
Jess giggles. "He is... Like, I can't deal with him."

Me: Us too. We can't wait for dinner tonight. Still not gonna tell us where we're going?
Hubby: I know you know what surprise means, kid...

I roll my eyes. "He's also super annoying."
Jess laughs out loud.

Me: Alright C.F. See you soon!
Hubby: *middle finger emoji*

Jess and I call Ben C.F. sometimes. It stands for... You guessed it.
Control freak.
After twenty more minutes of blasting Queen's Greatest Hits, Jessica and I arrive home. And we promptly start freaking out.
There are cars lining almost the entire street.
We gape at each other with wide eyes, pulling into the garage and hopping out of the truck to the sound of music, coming from the backyard.
"Oh my God!" Jess squeals, grabbing my arm and dragging me to the front door.
But when we get there, there's a sign taped on it that reads, *Husband and wife, please report to the backyard. Love, Ben Lockwood-Harper.*
Now we're both squealing.
Darting to the back gate, we open it and are met with an immediate wave of cheers and *Surprise!* I knew it was coming, but it still startles me.
Our smiles could be seen from outer space as we wave at all our closest friends and family, all gathered in the backyard for what looks to be an elaborate cookout party. There are decora-

tions everywhere, music playing and catered food. It's incredible.

Ben's up on the deck and he jumps down the steps two at a time to jog over to us. His smile is the cutest motherlovin' thing I've ever witnessed. Like humble pride, love and elation all wrapped up in one sexy as hell curve of the lips.

"Surprised?" He murmurs.

Jess leaps into his arms, holding onto him while he catches her, peppering his face and neck with kisses. And I hug onto his side, holding them both while we laugh together.

"I can't believe you did this," I whisper into his neck, acknowledging over his shoulder that I see my mom. *My mom!*

And my best friend ever and former roommate, Alec, with his girlfriend, Kayla. I haven't seen them in months, and was actually pretty bummed they weren't around for Pride since they still live in ABQ.

I feel like I could shed tears of joy, but I won't because that'd be embarrassing. But still...

"My mom, Alec and Kayla," I squeeze him tighter. "I'm drowning in my love for you right now."

Ben chuckles, "I'll give you mouth to mouth." Jess and I both laugh. "Happy anniversary, my loves."

"Happy anniversary," we tell him in unison, the three of us swooning together like a bunch of cornballs.

"Marrying you two changed my entire life," I breathe, pulling back to look at them. "Love doesn't even begin to cover it."

Jess pouts, grabbing my face and kissing me softly. When we part, I grab Ben's jaw and haul him to my lips, because I just need him.

When we finally pry ourselves apart, our guests are all waiting anxiously to greet us. And the gang really is all here. Jess's sister, Marie, and her husband, Greg. Ben and Jess's best friends, Bill and Rachel, Ben's brother, Jacob, his wife, Laura, and their twin girls.

My mom rushes us, giving me the giant, most suffocating hug ever. But honestly, it's so great to see her again. I can't believe she flew out from Colorado just for this party. Last time I saw her was almost a year ago, before Ethan was born.

"Oh my sweet darling boy," she breathes into the crook of my neck, her voice shaky with emotion. "I'm so happy to see you. And to *finally* meet that beautiful son of yours!"

My grin is wide with overwhelming emotion. "So you met Ethan?"

"I did! He's just perfect, sweetheart. Congratulations on this wonderful life you've built here with your new family." She pulls back and holds me at arm's length, eyes darting to Ben. I peek at him and he winks. "You have a great man, planning all of this and flying me out."

My eyes widen. "Ben flew you out?" I gawk at him again, and it seriously looks like there are hearts floating around his head.

"He did. He's perfect, baby. Just perfect." My mom pushes my hair back with her fingers. "And so is your beautiful wife!"

She leaves me to hug Jess for way too long, immediately launching into the baby conversation. I give Jess an apologetic look, but she brushes it off. I imagine she'll be stuck with Mom for a while, but Jess *is* perfect and sweet and adoring. I've been very fortunate.

My mother got along with Ben and Jess right away, the first time they met, and she always asks to speak with them on the phone when we talk. It's actually adorable.

But while Jess has Mom occupied, I dart over to my best friend, grabbing Alec and practically jumping on him. "I missed you so much!"

Alec laughs, embracing me just as hard. "Missed you too, Ry."

"Yea, we were so bummed we couldn't see you for Pride, but we knew we'd see you this weekend anyway," Kayla adds, and I go in for a huge hug from her next.

"So I guess Ben's been planning this for a while," I pull back, dazed, raking my fingers through my hair.

"Affirmative." Alec nods, folding his large tattooed arms over his chest. "He called us almost a month ago."

"You're very lucky, Ry-bear," Kayla grins.

"Oh my God, dude, we get it! Ben's hot," Alec teases, rolling his eyes.

"He is, though," I smirk at Kayla while wiggling my brows. "Come on. Let's go get a drink and you can tell me all about your trip to Vegas. I think I spy a bar set up over there."

"Oh yes, there is a bar, and there are some very interesting specialty cocktails," Alec grins.

My brows zip together, glancing at the bar, only to find people walking away with the penis drinks from Pride. Or at least something shockingly similar.

I burst out laughing, turning to Ben. He shrugs while inching closer to me.

"I couldn't resist," he takes my hand. "They were surprisingly delicious."

"Pervert." I lace our fingers.

"You know it."

I look around for a moment. "Hailey?"

"She's running late, but on her way," he tells me, bringing our joined hands to his lips to kiss mine.

I nod, excited beyond belief. "This is amazing, baby. You're like..."

"Fabulous?" He grins and fake-punch him in the kidney.

ABOUT AN HOUR LATER, I've already managed to down two *Cock*tails—*get it?*—and I'm working on my third while chatting with Alec, Greg and Bill about the Mustang. Well, we started talking about the Mustang, but somehow the conversation got here:

"So did you have an orgy at Pride?" Bill asks, sucking on the penis straw in his drink. It's a hilarious sight, I must say. This is probably why Ben added these drinks to the menu.

"Well, our relationship is only one person shy of an orgy as it is, *so*..." I shrug, and Alec dies laughing.

"I heard you guys ran into Tate," Greg says while inhaling an entire farm's worth of pigs in blankets. "Was that awkward?"

"I'm sure Ben made it awkward," Bill chuckles. And I have to laugh, because he's kind of right.

"You guys give Tate a hard time, but he's actually a great guy," I tell them. "I hope he can figure things out with that guy he likes. Lance something..."

Bill's eyes go wide. "You mean, the guy he liked in college? Lance Hardy?"

"Yea, I think that's the guy," I nod.

"He was there? At Pride??" Bill's face looks like he might explode. I've never known a straight guy who loves drama as much as Bill.

"Yea..." My forehead lines. "Why are you being weird?"

"That dude's *married*," Bill says, fully serious.

"Really?" More forehead creases. "Are you sure he's not like, getting a divorce or something?"

"No. He's still married, to a woman, and it seems like it's all good. At least according to their Facebook profiles."

"Yea well, social media doesn't always show the truth," I mutter.

"He's a Pastor," Greg mumbles through his chewing.

That one gets me. "*What??*"

Bill gasps, "Oh yea, I forgot about that! Yea, he's a Pastor at their church. United Methodist something or other."

"No, it's Presbyterian," Greg interjects.

"Who cares! You're saying not only is he a closeted gay guy who's married to a woman, but he's also a *Pastor??* That's crazy!"

"Yea, Tate sure does pick the wrong guys," Bill sighs.

"I'll say..." My mind is reeling.

I felt bad for Tate before, but now it's like, amplified. It must suck falling for someone you can't have like that...

Okay, been there done that.

"Babe!" Ben sidles over and grabs me by the waist. "Jacob just challenged me. I'm gonna need your assistance over there." He nods to where his brother is tossing a football up in the air.

I grin. "Just like old times, huh?"

Ben nods with enthusiasm. "Let's go."

We go to the far end of the yard and start passing the ball back and forth. The rest of the guys join us, but we're mostly just goofing around. And it's fun.

Ben, the former football prodigy, schools everyone, but I'm almost as good. I love adding a little healthy competition into our relationship. It's almost like foreplay. Seriously, watching him gets me hard, as does letting him boss me around.

It's one of my many fantasies. He's the hot quarterback who likes to get fucked by his wide receiver in the showers. *Yumm, I fuckin need it.*

I catch one of Ben's all-star passes, darting away from him while he chases me all over the place. He catches me and pulls me to him, both of us out of breath and feeling the sexual tension like a current between us. And just as I think we might need to sneak off for a quick blowy in the shed, I hear someone shout, "Hailey!"

Ben and I look up to find Hailey walking into the backyard, blonde hair flowing just like her beautiful floral dress, on the arm of my former Sociology professor, Oliver Morrison.

Aka, her new boyfriend.

The first thing I do is look at Ben. I can't imagine he extended the invitation to Oliver, which is confirmed by the look of shock on his face. Hailey finds Jess first, giving her a massive hug. Oliver hands our wife a bottle of wine, smiling and polite in his outfit that makes him look like a Harvard alum going for a sail.

Ben begins stomping over to them, holding my hand in a death grip, which means he's *dragging* me along.

"Hi, Daddy!" Hailey smiles, giving Ben a hug, before moving to me. "Ryan! Happy anniversary!"

"Thanks," I mutter weakly, feeling the tension thicken in the air like smog.

"You guys remember Oliver," she gestures to Professor Morrison, whose smile is a bit wary as he extends a hand to Ben.

Ben shakes it with his left so he can keep squeezing mine with his right.

After that, no one says anything for what feels like an eternity, though in actuality it's no more than ten seconds.

"I didn't know you'd be bringing a date," Ben finally grumbles, giving Oliver a studious once-over.

"Yea well, it worked out so well last time, I figured I'd give bringing a guy home another shot," Hailey grins.

Ben pales.

I choke.

Oliver chuckles. "Yes, don't go falling in love with me now." When Ben's eyes nearly bug out of his head and my face turns the shade of Satan's asshole, the professor backtracks. "I'm sorry. My sense of humor often leaves much to be desired. Obviously I have no intention of um... Never mind."

"Jesus take the wheel," I mutter to myself as Jess saunters over with a drink in her hand.

"What are we talking about?" She smiles.

Hailey blinks a few times before I respond, "Nothing much."

"Nothing much," Ben repeats, sounding like he's broken.

"Wow, Hailey, you've got guts, huh?" Bill stumbles over, clearly half in the bag, looking all disheveled. "Bringing *another* guy home!" He lets a drunk giggle slip before looking to Oliver. "Hey, pal, whatever you do, don't spend the night!"

Jess's face freezes, before she turns to our friend, glaring at him until he looks terrified. I can practically hear her telepathically threatening his life.

"Anyway!" Hailey shouts, tugging Oliver closer to her by his arm. "I just wanted you guys to get to know Ol a little bit better since he's very important to me." She pauses and blinks. "I mean, not *get to know* him, like that, but like... Just as my boyfriend. Not yours."

Bill snickers and I cover my face with my free hand. *This has to be the most awkward moment of my entire life.*

"For fuck's sake," Ben barks. "We're not animals, okay? We can control ourselves. Ryan was an isolated incident, brought on by something like... fate or whatever."

"Ben, please..." I mutter, shaking from the sheer uncomfortableness of this conversation.

"Hailey, I love you," he sighs. "You're my daughter, and

you're the most important thing in my life. That said, your man's not even that cute. Boom."

"Ben!" Jess gasps out loud, the eyeballs fully exiting her skull.

"Excuse me?" Hailey growls, partly in amusement, though there looks to be a hint of disbelief on her face.

"Can we please stop..." I whimper, trying to tug my hand out of Ben's so I can flee, though he just grips tighter.

"Oliver is a ten, Dad," Hailey's arms fold over her chest and she pops out her hip in that way she does when she's trying to win an argument. We've all seen it before.

"I'm glad you feel that way, sweetheart," Ben gives her a condescending smile.

"I can't believe you're saying he's not!" Hailey gasps.

"Hails, your man is very attractive. Okay?" I gripe. "Now, who wants a drink?! Or five. I'm buying!"

"Are you saying you want me to think he's hot?" Ben's head cocks.

Hailey freezes, remaining quiet for a moment before she answers. "No..."

"Okay then. Great," Ben grins. "So we're all on the same page. Now, how about some food? Oliver, you hungry? We've got steak, fish or chicken, of all different varieties. Come on."

Ben finally lets go of my hand, motioning for Oliver to follow him.

"Um... thank you?" Oliver shoots Hailey a look, visibly glad he survived that little ordeal, though the nerves are clearly still there.

"You like scotch?" Ben asks as they leave.

"I'm really more of a gin man," Oliver replies warily.

"See? It could never work between us," Ben turns to give Hailey a wink before taking her new boyfriend off to do God knows what.

Well, we know one thing they won't be doing... Going to the basement!

"I feel like he's fallen off the deep end," Hailey sighs, then looks at me. "I blame you."

"Me?!" I laugh. Then she laughs.

Then we all laugh, and I say a silent prayer, thanking God for an end to that awkwardness. Because honestly, if human beings could die from embarrassment, I'd be in a body bag right now.

Jess and I decide to go check on Ethan, who's currently being passed around between Laura, my mom, Rachel, Marie and a few other friends who are going completely gaga over our adorable child. Then we end up making out in a closet for a few minutes because, why the hell not?

Creeping back out to the party, visibly guilty and fixing ourselves up, we come face to face with someone I was entirely unaware Ben invited...

Tate.

"Hey, it's the new and improved Lockwoods," he grins, leaning in to kiss our cheeks. "Great party."

"Did you just get here?" I ask and he nods.

"Yea, just now."

I laugh. "You wanna go get a drink?"

"Sure," he shrugs, then looks around and leans in, "But I'd rather go see the shed. If you know what I mean." He winks.

I give him an odd look, but Jess beats me to the question. "What are you talking about?"

His brow arches. "You know... the *film setting*, if you will."

Oh no. I immediately realize what he's referring to and hold my hand up, motioning for him to shut up, but he either can't understand what I'm trying to say, or he doesn't care, because he keeps talking.

"I gotta hand it to you, you've got balls, Harper. I mean,

sure, you don't know for a fact that anyone you know watches gay porn, but if they secretly do? Your video would pop right up. I mean, it's slaying Pornhub right now, and trust me, I watch a lot of it. So I would know."

My heart is jumping like crazy while Jess turns her confused expression on me. Sweat is lining my brow. *I'm gonna be in so much trouble.*

"Ryan..." Jess mutters, blinking over wide blue eyes. "Please tell me you didn't..."

My mouth opens to respond, but it's not going to be the answer she wants, so I physically can't say anything.

"You didn't!" She gasps, shoving me in the chest. "That video was supposed to be just for us! And now you're telling me my husbands are porn stars?!"

"*Amateur* porn stars," Tate corrects. "But with the right lighting, I think you guys could do great things."

"How many times have you watched us fuck now, hm?" I hiss at Tate, trying desperately to keep my voice down, since there are people everywhere.

"Stop fucking for the whole world to see then!" He counters with a brow raise.

"Oh my God," Jess huffs, half laughing, half mortified. "Pornhub, Ryan. Porn fucking Hub. I can't..."

"What's on Pornhub?"

All of our heads spring in the direction of Ben as he rounds the corner with Oliver and Hailey right behind him. He's staring at me and Jess, waiting for us to answer him, but I'm just frozen solid. *How much awkwardness can I endure in one day?? Jesus.*

"Hm... This oughta be interesting." Tate leans up against the wall, crossing his arms over his chest like he's preparing for a show.

I can't help but seethe at him silently before I turn back to my husband. I guess it's time to come clean. And really, doing so in front of his daughter is the definition of an awful idea, but after the shitshow he forced me into outside earlier, I'd say we're already past the point of no return.

"Okay, don't be mad," I breathe, placing a hand on Ben's chest, "But I... kinda... sorta... put that, um," my eyes dart to Hailey and my voice lowers, "*Video* we made... up on Pornhub."

Ben looks sufficiently shocked, and an, "Oh snap," comes from Oliver, to which we all glare in his direction.

"Okay, I think this is our cue to go literally anywhere but here," Hailey grumbles, grabbing the professor and tugging him away from what seems like a reality show he's rather invested in.

"Please don't lose respect for us, sweetie!" Jess calls after her, giving me a fiery look.

"I'm sorry..." Ben blinks. "You said you put that video... the one we made the other day... on the biggest online porn warehouse of all time?"

My blinking becomes rapid, my palms sweating as I nod. "It already has over twenty-thousand views."

"Most of them were him," Jess teases, nodding in Tate's direction.

Ben turns to glare at Tate, "Can you make yourself scarce? This is a family matter."

"Sure thing..." Tate murmurs, pushing off the wall to leave us, but not without first muttering, "*Daddy.*" And throwing Ben a wink.

Ben is seething. I can *feel* it.

"I could strangle you to death for that reason alone!" He gestures in the direction Tate just went.

"Baby, I'm *sorry*," I mumble and move in closer, brushing his neck with my fingers in a shameless effort to distract him from his anger. "It's just that it was so hot, and honestly... it's kind of a fantasy of mine."

"To make porn?" He growls, narrowing a bristling blue gaze at me.

"Amateur porn," Jess grins.

He pins her with a look. "You're not helping."

"To do it with you..." I whisper. "I didn't think anyone we knew would see it. Since, you know..."

"Uh, we know Tate!" Ben whisper-shouts. "He probably watches gay porn more than he eats!" I can't help but giggle, covering it up with my fingers on my lips. "Not funny, troublemaker."

"I'm sorry. I know I should have told you, but I just wanted to try it. I blurred our faces! Or at least, I tried to. I'm not great at that stuff, I'll admit..."

"Lord have mercy..." Ben grumbles, running his fingers through his hair. He chews on his lip for a moment while I gaze at him, giving him my best puppy dog eyes. "So... twenty-thousand views?"

His eyes meet mine, and there's still a bit of scolding in them. But his soft lips are curving into the slightest grin, which I have to appreciate.

"It's like... amazing," I lean in, kissing his neck.

"To be honest, I've always had a fantasy of messing around with porn stars," Jess chuckles as Ben pulls her into his side. "So this is a win-win for me."

"I hate both of you," Ben laughs.

"C.F. didn't lose his mind," I mutter to Jess through my massive grin. "I totally thought he would."

"C.F. is gonna spank your ass tonight, kid," Ben rumbles, kissing me softly, then grasping Jess's face to do the same.

"Make sure you record it," she laughs.

CHAPTER SEVEN
Jessica

By the time everyone's stumbling out of our party, it's after one in the morning.

Ryan's besties, Alec and Kayla are staying overnight in the guest room, since they live in ABQ and I wouldn't dream of having them drive home for hours at night. Believe it or not, much to all of our relief, Hailey opted to stay in a hotel with her boyfriend, rather than at the house.

I think it's still a sensitive subject. Maybe it always will be, but there's nothing we can do to change it. As long as we stay open and honest, it'll work out. It has to.

Laura's spending the night as well to tend to Ethan so that Ryan, Ben and I can have our alone time. I've never been more grateful.

Because after that great party, and all the cocktails consumed over the course of it, the three of us have become a bit keyed up.

I linger back in the house, saying goodnight to the baby while Ben and Ryan get started in the hot tub. It's necessary for no other reason than I want to sneak up on them and watch for a minute or two.

I'm not even lying when I tell you it's my favorite thing. When I watched that video they recorded the other day—the one that apparently made them up-and-coming stars of Pornhub—I came four times *by myself*, before I even made it to either of them. There's nothing quite like watching the two of them together. Without even mentioning how mind-numbingly gorgeous they both are, their chemistry is unlike anything I could even put into words.

It has a mind of its own, hence the occasional role changes and apparent Daddy kink, which I'm one-hundred percent onboard with, by the way.

So making my way out to our new secluded hot tub area, I'm shivering with anticipation. I've left them alone for about fifteen minutes, which is more than enough time for them to get started. It doesn't take much with those two. And sure enough, when I round the corner of the shed and peer in between the wall of plants and trees, I see exactly what I was hoping for.

They're both in the hot tub, and it looks like they're naked, which is lovely. Ben is leaning up against the side, on one of the seats with Ryan on his lap, and they're kissing. They're doing that slow-burn kiss they do, when it's obvious that it feels just way too good to rush. My inner walls are throbbing already as I watch with wide eyes, Ryan's hands taking in the feel of Ben's shoulders and chest. Then Ryan leans back a bit, enough for Ben's mouth to trail his throat down to his chest, sucking his nipples until Ryan's audibly panting.

"I love what you do to me," Ryan breathes with his hands in Ben's hair.

"I love how hard I can make your big dick," Ben growls, reaching just beneath the surface of the water to grip Ryan's cock.

And that's enough of the watching.

I wander over to them, immediately tearing my clothes off. I love how dim the lights are in here. The contractors did an amazing job. It truly feels like we're in this little rainforest sex shack; somewhere built entirely for hot fucking and the best possible erotic ambiance.

Ben's eyes meet mine, but he keeps going on Ryan's nipples, sucking while stroking him in the water. Ryan's hooded gaze locks on me as well, biting his lip while he watches me, completely naked, stepping into the hot tub with them.

We also made sure to get a model with all sorts of range as far as temperature settings go. We wanted something we could use all year round, and right now it's definitely set to a cooler temperature, since it's still warm outside. It's refreshing, and also brings an immediate heat to my face. Well, that and watching what my husbands are doing to each other.

And the jets. *Yes, God bless the jets.*

"Hi," Ryan reaches out and pulls me over. I go to them without hesitation, wasting no time kissing him, then Ben.

"I can't believe it's been a year since Thailand," Ben hums in my mouth.

"I know," I go for Ryan's neck, holding Ben's shoulder while I kiss everywhere.

"Best time ever," Ryan whispers.

"Remember the honeymoon?" I grin and they both chuckle, deviously.

"I remember you lost your voice from screaming," Ben smirks.

"I better not have a voice tomorrow, or you guys are slacking," I grin.

They share a look, brows cocking before Ryan says, "Challenge accepted. Ben..." Ryan nods at him and Ben immediately hops up out of the tub, sitting at the edge, his beautiful dick standing tall in all its glory.

Ryan winks at me, and I go in first, taking Ben in my mouth, sucking him slow and deep, the way he likes it. The sounds he makes have to be the most lascivious music to my ears, not to mention he has such a perfectly *filthy* mouth.

"Suck deep, wife," he growls, wrapping my hair around his fist. "Take this cock all the way down and swallow it."

I'm dizzy by the time Ryan lifts me up and practically deposits me on Ben's lap. I straddle his hips and he wastes no time pushing me down on his dick, burying himself deep within my walls until I'm purring.

"Tight, warm pussy," he cups my tits, holding them while I ride him. "You're like silk squeezing my cock, babe."

"Yes... *Ben*," I grip his chest right back, moving up and down, building a rhythm.

All of a sudden, I feel Ryan's hot breath beneath my ass. He grips me with his strong hands, helping me ride Ben while he licks my pussy and Ben's dick, underneath us. It's fucking intense, feeling him licking my lips, tongue swirling around Ben's shaft in between thrusts.

"I fucking love his mouth," Ben rumbles, holding my face and kissing me deep, hauling me forward so Ryan can really get in there.

"Ryan..." I whimper.

"Yea, baby?" He rasps, sounding every bit as fuzzy as I feel.

"I want your cock in me," I plead, dropping my head to Ben's chest.

"Anything for you," he whispers.

He moves up behind me, kneeling on the step before lifting me off Ben's cock and depositing me on his. Then he rumbles in my ear, "I just need to get some of this lube first." A soft mewl leaves my lips while he kisses the nape of my neck, thrusting up into me while circling my clit with his thumb. "Ben, suck on her tits."

Ben doesn't need to be asked twice. He leans forward, his giant erection writhing against my belly while he sucks my nipples, right, then left, then right, then left, nipping at them until I'm coming undone.

Ryan fucks me slowly for only a couple more minutes before he puts me back on Ben's dick, spreads open my ass and presses his dick between my cheeks. "Relaxed?"

He always asks, though we've done this more times than I can count. But he has to double-check because he's precious, and there's seriously no one like him in the entire world. Ryan Harper is pure perfection.

I nod eagerly, leaning back against his solid chest. "Put your big dick in my ass, baby."

"God, I love you." Ryan gives it a nice push.

And I spontaneously combust.

It's seriously the most fantastically full feeling ever invented. They just sandwich me like I'm a piece of cheese between two slices of the hottest bread.

I'm on Ben's chest, writhing into him while he holds my ass open, for leverage for himself, but also for Ryan. And Ryan's thrusts match Ben's immaculately, his chest covering my back. I'm seeing stars, the two of them grinding into me together, holding me, and each other.

Ryan's hand comes up to hold Ben's neck while he breathes on my nape, and I think Ben's actually running the fingers of his free hand between Ryan's ass cheeks.

It's all just so much, and I know I'm going to come any moment.

They keep going, keep fucking me together, creating overwhelming sensations all over my body. From the both of them inside me, dicks meeting through the wall of my pussy, to my clit rubbing on Ben's pelvis and my hardened nipples on his chest, to Ryan's moans ghosting breaths over my back... It's all just... *stupefying*.

I begin tightening all over, and of course they can feel it.

"You gonna come, baby?" Ben groans, taking over a bit while Ryan's stroking slows.

"Yes," I nod frantically. "Yes yes *yes*."

"Soak me, Jessica," he demands, running a hand up to my breast and flicking my nipple.

For some reason, it sets me off.

I erupt like a volcano in Pompei, crying out nonsense onto the flesh of Ben's throat while they both hold me tight, cradling my shivering body between them. As soon as I'm done, Ryan pulls out of my ass slowly.

"You want next, beautiful?" He gasps, and I know he's talking to Ben.

"Fuck me," Ben demands, shuddering when Ryan pushes up to his ass. "Fuck... *me*..."

"You love this dick, don't you?" Ryan groans, holding me in between them while he spreads Ben's legs wider, thrusting into him deeper and deeper. "You both do."

"I love it," I pick back up riding Ben's cock while Ryan takes him for his own ride.

"Me too," Ben grunts. "Right there... Baby, pound me. I want it hard."

"Anything for you," Ryan's voice is hoarse as his thrusts become rougher, draping himself over me while he pumps into Ben with all his strength.

I'm going out of my mind, winding up again, my sensitive clit ready to let me dance in euphoria once more as my body grips Ben's dick and refuses to let go.

"She fucking loves it as much as I do," Ben's head lolls back, then the rest of his torso until he's practically lying on the ground, with my riding his hips and his legs spread for Ryan. "Her pussy gets crazy tight and juicy when you fuck me."

Ryan pulls Ben's calf up by his head. "Jess, you want him to come in your pussy, or your mouth? Cuz I'm gonna make him bust in like five seconds."

"*Fuuuckk...*" Ben's eyes are rolling back in his head.

And my body launches into this insane orgasm that feels like a train of aching tingles is caboosing through my insides. I can't even recognize myself while I gasp for air. I'm all sensation as I tug myself out from in between them, making a quick shuffle of turning around so I can suck Ben's cock.

Literally the second my mouth closes around his head, he starts coming.

"Fuck... fuck fuck fuck..." Is the only thing he can say as he pulses down my throat.

"That's it, baby," Ryan caresses his chest, his thrusts slowing down considerably. "You come so good. Like a dream, love."

"Come inside me," Ben's love drunk voice rasps, cheeks all pink and flushed, the wall of his muscled chest moving with his breaths.

"I'm already there," Ryan gasps, then he tumbles over. Last but never least.

I pop off Ben's cock and Ryan falls forward into his arms, kissing him deep while he murmurs about filling him up. I can stop touching either of them, my fingers trailing their lines while Ben pulls me close.

As usual, we're a big pile of limbs and sweat and sex, our hair all over the place, breaths echoing off the trees.

"You know, we're still outside," Ben chuckles, fingers trailing up and down both of our backs. "This isn't a soundproof area."

"Yea our neighbors hate us," I giggle.

"They already thought we were deviants before," Ryan grins. "Now they're in for a real treat."

Ryan pulls out of Ben, then the three of us cuddle up together, at the edge of our new hot tub, kissing and touching for minutes on end. And it's beautiful.

It's perfect.

It's *us*.

It's Sunday afternoon.

Laura left earlier, but Hailey came over and she and Oliver have spent the day with Ethan.

I know Ben had his initial doubts, but the guy is actually super nice. He's polite, charming, educated... British. I mean, what more could a parent want for their daughter?

Plus, she tried bringing home a boy her own age before, and we all remember how that played out. *Forever LOLing.*

I think Ben got over his aversion to Professor Morrison last night, during the party. According to him, they talked, shared a drink, and did some guy bonding or whatever, very different from the bonding Ben did with Ryan last Thanksgiving. *The jokes are there, guys. I can't not make them.*

Whatever they talked about, I'm glad they seemed to work things out. All we really want is for Hailey to be happy. And even if this thing with Oliver ends up fizzling out, she's twenty years old. Now is the time when she'll experience life, date guys, make mistakes. It's part of the process, the part of growing up that Ben and I never quite reached, until we met Ryan.

He gave us a renewed happily ever after.

Ryan is in the garage with Alec, who's helping him get the new seats into the Mustang. Ben's showing Kayla the garden while Hailey and Oliver traipse around the yard with Ethan, making him laugh like the happy baby he is.

And I'm just... *breathing*.

All this love, all this family... It'll never go away. I'm more content than I've ever been in my life, and I have all these people to thank, but most importantly... My husbands. Both so different in their own ways, and yet the other pieces of my heart.

The smile refuses to leave my face, even as the doorbell rings and I go to answer it.

I pull open the door to find a large man with blonde hair gazing down at me. He looks concerned, which is odd because I've never been happier. *I figured it'd be contagious.*

"Hi, can I help you?" I ask, peering to the left at Ryan and Alec, laughing in the driveway.

"Um... I'm sorry," the man says, and now that I'm taking a deeper look at him, he appears stressed and tired. "This is really weird, but... I'm looking for Tate Eckhart."

I blink a few times up at the man who's easily a foot taller than me. "And uh... who are you?"

"Lance?" Ryan walks up behind the guy with Alec at his side.

"Ohhh... *you're* Lance?" It's all making sense.

This is Tate's college crush.

But why is he here?

"Yea, um, hi," Lance addresses Ryan, still a bit stiff and apparently uncomfortable. "I've been trying to reach Tate, but haven't been able to get a hold of him. His assistant said he was coming to Tularosa for the weekend, and I know you guys are his friends..."

"Stalker," Alec coughs, and Ryan elbows him.

"What's going on over here?" Ben wanders in from the backyard, Kayla, Hailey, Oliver and Ethan in tow. "Oh, hey. Lance, right?"

"Yea, uh... this is super awkward," Lance shakes his head, turning away from me. "I should just go."

"Whoa whoa, don't leave," I call to him. "Tate was here last night. Usually he stays at my in-laws when he comes to Tularosa." I look to Ben. "Is Tate at Jake's?"

Ben looks a little skeptical. "I'm not sure if we should be telling him these things. I mean, if you want to see Tate, couldn't you just call him?"

"He's ignoring my calls," Lance says with pain in his voice. "But I really need to speak with him."

"Well, if he's ignoring you then I'm sure he doesn't want to speak with you," Ben murmurs.

"Uh, hate to interject here," Alec steps forward, "But weren't you doing this exact thing at my house in ABQ last New Years?"

"Alec," Kayla gasps, then squeezes Ben's arm, rolling her eyes to him. "Oh my God, he's so embarrassing."

I let a giggle slip. "He's right, Ben. What about when this was you looking for Ryan?"

"Awww," Ryan pouts. "So sweet."

"It was really sweet," Hailey says, poking Ethan's nose.

"Alright alright, Jesus," Ben grunts. "Don't you people forget anything?" He pulls his phone out of his pocket. "I'll get to the bottom of this." He presses a button and brings the phone to his ear, all of us staring at him in silence. "Tate? Hey, man. How's it going?"

Lance starts making all kinds of gestures to Ben and Ben waves him off, turning away.

"Look uh... Are you at my brother's?" Ben asks Tate on the phone. We're all leaning in, anxious for some more of this juicy gossip, like a live action episode of *Jersey Shore* or something. Ben nods at Lance and gives him a thumbs up. "Oh, nice. So just wondering... that guy Lance... what's up with you two?"

Ben puts the phone on speaker. "Lockwood, is this your way of asking if I'm single? Because trust me, what with my history with your husband, I really don't think it's a good idea..."

Alec and Kayla snort out a laugh, Oliver looks sufficiently disturbed and Ryan pushes forward.

"Um hello, Tate," Ryan barks into the phone. "My husband is not hitting on you."

"Oh hi, Ryan!" Tate croons into the phone.

"Hey. So this guy Lance—"

"Oh my God, whatever you do, don't tell him where I am," Tate says. And everyone's eyes dart to Lance. "I'm trying to freeze him out so he gets the hint. I'm a fucking idiot and I can't chase straight closeted guys anymore. It's like beyond fucking toxic."

We're all quiet for a moment, gaping at Lance. He looks immensely distraught, and I have an overwhelming desire to wrap a blanket around him and give him cocoa.

"Tate..." Lance says, his voice almost audibly shivering.

"Oh fuck," Tate sighs into the phone. "Dude, boundaries. I can't believe you came all the way down here!"

"I'm sorry. I just..." his voice trails and he looks at us nervously. The poor thing is obviously so shy. He grabs the phone out of Ben's hand and turns away. "I needed to see you."

Tate is quiet for a moment. That on its own is fascinating. Tate Eckhart doesn't get flustered or choked up.

"Why?" He finally mutters through the phone.

"To say that I'm sorry..." Lance rakes his fingers through his hair. "And to tell you that I've been... thinking about you. About us."

"Yea, I told you, that's not—"

"I mean before," Lance interrupts. "I was thinking about you before I saw you at Pride. For like... a while."

"Awww," I whisper, pulling Ryan close to me. We both pout at each other because seriously...

Is there anything better than the moment the unsure guy finally admits his feelings??

"Tell him he's forgiven, Tate!" Hailey shouts toward the phone.

"Yea, accept the love!" Kayla adds, squeezing onto Alec.

Lance gives them both a look like they're insane.

"You guys don't get it, okay?" Tate mumbles, sounding more uneasy than I've ever heard him before. "It's not that simple..."

"Can we at least talk?" Lance pleads.

"No." Tate grumbles.

"Tate, I'm already out here," Lance sighs. "I drove for over five hours on the off-chance I might be able to track you down. I won't stop until you agree to see me."

"Okay, that's really fuckin sweet," Ben sighs, looking to Ryan and me, all three of us pouting at each other now.

"Jesus Christ, fine!" Tate hisses. "Anything to get rid of the audience commentary. I'll text you the address."

"Thank you, T," Lance finally smiles, and it's, like, a *really* beautiful one. You can tell he's the guy who doesn't do it often, and for a reason. Because they're that special. "I can't wait to see you."

"Yea yea." Tate hangs up and Lance hands the phone back to Ben, grin still present on his lips.

"Thank you guys so much for your help," he breathes.

"Hey, we believe in love here," Ben winks, pulling me and Ryan closer.

Lance stomps down the walkway, waving at us as he goes back to his car. And we wave back.

Hailey rests her head on Oliver's shoulder. "I hope it works out for them."

Ryan turns his face to Ben and me, giving us a knowing smile. "Me too."

THE VACATION

CHAPTER ONE
Ben

Head back. Eyes closed. Warmth seeping into every crevice of my muscles, tight and hot. Sweet *sweet* comfort.

It feels so good. Much needed. And wonderful.

"Papa!"

My eyes roll. I can't help it. They just do.

I was having such a nice time relaxing in my hot tub. Well-deserved silence for once in a great while, I carved out a spot in my crazy day, between work and supporting my beautiful family, coming home to be with Ethan and the loves of my life, then slinking off to bed for adult play time, which is beyond delicious, but let's be real…it's not quiet or calm in any way shape or form.

I don't get much of this, so when I do get, I savor it. I hold on tight and squeeze because God only knows… as much as I love my life more than even imaginable, I sometimes miss the quiet.

Jess and I were all set for early retirement before Ethan came along. And he's the best unexpected blessing ever, besides his daddy of course. My son is fantastic, and truly a low maintenance kid.

But still... I'm almost thirty eight, and I haven't yet been able to reap any of the benefits of teenage pregnancy.

Sure, there was the Thailand vacation before Ethan was born. And then the epic Pride weekend over the summer. But at this point we've been back in the fold of regular life for months.

Schedules and meetings and plans with friends and play dates for Ethan and all the stuff that sometimes makes me forget I'm in a throuple with my wife and our daughter's ex-boyfriend.

It's a hard fact to forget. *Especially when your friends remind you constantly.*

But right now, soaking in the beautiful hot tub my husband and wife got me for our anniversary while my adorable one-year-old squeals, having awoken from his half-hour nap that seems to have blown by in an eye-blink, I'm having a little craving. I'm feeling the unsettling desire deep in my bones again...

We need a vacation.

"Papa!" Ethan, rather dramatically, shrieks once more from his play pen.

And I sigh out loud, hoisting myself up out of the hot tub to attend to him, ending once and for all what was supposed to be a relaxing hour of Ben time.

"Okay, buddy," I kneel down next to him, lifting him out of the pen where he's holding himself up on the side. "Papa's here."

Ethan giggles, warming my chest a thousand times more than that hot tub ever could, reaching up to touch my face with his tiny hand. His smile really rounds out his chubby cheeks, teal eyes sparkling up at me while he coos his version of words, telling his father a story. And I think I can understand it...

"I love you too, buddy." I grin, standing up to swing him around the way he loves. "You like spending time with Papa, huh?"

His full-bellied baby laughs give me all the satisfaction I need. This kid is worth it... All of it. All the inconveniences of parenting late in the game, every time in the middle of the night I hear his tiny sad whimpers while I'm knee deep in my wife, or on my back with my legs in the air and my hair in my husband's fist... It's all good because Ethan is the reason we're even here.

If Jess hadn't gotten pregnant two years ago, who knows if the three of us would have found our ways back together?

He's a little blessing baby, which is why I'm so glad he looks so much like Ryan. I mean, it's still a toss-up as far as which of us is genetically his father, since he seems to have my nose and chin.

Honestly, I'd be more than happy to find out my son has my husband's genes. But Ryan and Jess don't want to know, and I get it. He's *ours* regardless of the blood swimming in his veins.

"Oh, bud," I chuckle, "You're *way* too peaceful right now. You jacked up my quiet time, now it's only fair I return the favor."

Lifting his tiny t-shirt, I bring my lips to his fat belly and blow, doing the best raspberries around until he's damn near hyperventilating he's giggling so hard.

"God, I love that sound," my wife's voice interrupts Ethan's laughter and I glance up to find her walking onto the patio, smiling wide, blue eyes locked on our adorable son.

"Love the sight, too," Ryan murmurs, following behind her

with his evergreen eyes set on me. He tugs his lower lip between his teeth and I growl.

"Don't make that face at me while I'm holding a child." His lips curve into a wicked smirk and I whisper to Ethan, "Daddy's being fresh."

"What else is new?" Jess chuckles, then reaches for Ethan. "Gimme gimme."

I laugh and hand our son over, kissing her cheek before sidling up to Ryan and kissing his jaw. But before I can back up, he grabs mine.

"More, baby," he breathes, and I don't need any begging.

I kiss his lower lip slowly while he purrs. Then I suck it into my mouth and he melts into me.

It goes on for only about ten seconds, but when we pull apart we're both a lil hazy.

With my hands on his chest, I peek at my wife, who's grinning up a storm. "You want me to take him inside for a few before I start dinner?"

My eyes slink back to Ryan whose gaze is hooded with lust. But still he clears his throat and mumbles, "No, it's um...okay. I have work to do."

I have to crush my smile before it gets crazy. Ryan and I haven't had alone time in a few weeks. Now, that's not to say we don't have our fun together... I don't think even prison could separate us. *We'd find a way.*

But lately, it's been the three of us together every night, doing our sexy thing. Ethan's sleep schedule has smoothed out a bit, but I just took on two new jobs that have had me working relatively late nights and some weekends. The abundance of time we had early on in our relationship has sort of dissipated and now we're left with only evenings.

That and Jessica is still clearly trying to make up for the

fact that she couldn't get tossed around for months while she was pregnant.

It's been fun as all hell, don't get me wrong. We have a blast, always. But every once in a while, I'll get the look from my husband that I'm getting right now... The one that says *I need to be on my knees behind you in the shed.*

We try to have separate date nights between the three of us. We think it's important in a throuple. Jess and I just had one last week, which is probably why she's offering to take Ethan and give me some time with my man.

But Ryan's also been crazy busy lately.

He sold the Mustang he rebuilt and bought a GTO. The thing is in great condition, but it needs a lot of work. So now it's back to the beginning of his process which is by far the busiest.

Tapping his chin with my knuckles, I shoot him a wink, then pat him on the butt. "Go get 'em, tiger."

"Put me in the game, coach," he teases with a grin.

"If that's the role playing you guys are doing this time, I expect another video," Jess says. When I peek at her, she wiggles her eyebrows. "Thank youuu."

Ryan laughs out loud. "Oh don't you remember, babe? We've retired from the porn game." His eyes dart to mine. "*Daddy* said one was enough." His lips curl wickedly, and I squint at him.

"First of all, when he's around, you're Daddy." I nod at Ethan. "And second of all, don't poke the bear, kid. If you'll recall, it's been far too long since I've given you rug burn."

He's trying to act tough, but I can *see* him shivering. I suddenly have way too much saliva in my mouth.

"I say again, should I take this baby out of here?" Jess asks once more, grinning, though she's fully serious.

"I do have work to do," Ryan pouts. His forest green eyes shimmer up at me as he whispers, "But how about tonight?"

I want to drop to my knees and weep at his feet for it. Alone time with Ryan is like a drug for me. And I'm itching like a fiend.

But then... It's much more fun to play with him.

So I simply brush my lips over his ear and whisper, "We'll see."

I drop a kiss behind it, and then I'm sauntering away, into the shed to dry off and get dressed.

I don't need to look back to know he's gawking at my ass like a Thanksgiving feast.

Ryan

W<small>HIRRING</small>, *whirring, whirring.*

I'm gliding my wet-sander along the fender of the GTO, gently grinding down some of the imperfections so I can repaint.

It's fun. I think this is actually my favorite part of the restore, other than picking out the interior.

The mechanics are a bitch, but that's why I bought this one. Its guts are perfect. It just needs a little makeover.

Okay, maybe a big makeover.

But still, I'm enjoying it. I never thought I could make something like this into a career, but here I am...

Twenty-three and living the dream.

Thing is, right now I'm having trouble focusing because the *whirring* of this machine in my hands, the way it's sort of vibrating while I drag it along the curve of the fender...

I swallow in a gulp. *My dick is hard.*

Turning off the wet-sander and lifting my goggles up, I let out a long breath. My husband is such a sexy tease, I swear to God.

He knew he was getting me all riled up earlier, on top of the riling that's already been happening since the last time we had our alone time.

And yes, we fuck on the regular because there's absolutely no way we ever wouldn't. But the thing about me and Ben is that our chemistry is a living thing. Like an organism that spreads between us, hungry and insistent.

It's always been this way. I have absolutely no idea where it came from, or how it's even possible... But if that first weekend we met is any indication, we were always destined to hump each other's brains out.

It was written in the stars.

So even though our wife and I shared his dick like a milkshake with two straws last night, I'm still on edge and itching for more.

The *alone time*, like we had at Pride.

My gaze goes across the room to my workbench, where I have a bunch of pictures hanging up.

One is of the three of us at Pride. Another shows the three of us in Thailand on our wedding night. And then there's the one Jess took of Ben and me in the infinity pool a couple days after the wedding.

I can't help the nostalgic sigh that leaves my lips as I think back to that magical time.

Thailand was fantastic. I mean, not only were we all blissfully basking in the fact that we were back together, for real that time. But also it was just the most gorgeous, relaxing tropical setting I've ever experienced.

Not that I've been to many places... *Okay, maybe it's the only place I've been.* But still. It was unforgettable.

Any place that can drive you to get spur-of-the-moment married I think puts something in the water.

A few more hours go by, and suddenly it's dark outside the garage and even with my space-heater on, I'm freezing. Glancing at the clock, I notice that it's well after dinner time.

Shit... I hope Jess won't be mad. Although I'm sure if she wanted us to eat together, she would have come to get me.

Wandering inside the house, I follow the smell of food into the kitchen. Ethan is sitting in his highchair with something that looks like mashed carrot on his face. He squeals when I come into the room, a word that's almost *Dada*, but not quite there yet.

He's only mastered *Papa* so far, which is reserved for Ben, and *Ma*, which is obviously Jess. Though sometimes he says it to me, which I'll admit, I don't love.

"Hey, Prince Ethan," I grin at him, sidling over to kiss his head and try to clean him up, while Jess is obviously busy rinsing dishes and stuffing them into the dishwasher. "Why didn't you come get me?"

She gives me a tired smile over her shoulder. "You were in the zone. I saved you a plate. It's in the microwave."

Wiping the last of the orange mush off my son's face, I walk over to my wife and move her blonde hair to the side, giving her a few soft neck kisses. "Where's Ben?"

"He had some work to finish up." She turns off the water and dries her hands, spinning in my arms. "Here's what I want."

"Tell me."

She drapes her hands on my chest, gazing up at me with

those ocean eyes. "I want you to eat your dinner. In the living room, even. That way you can put your feet up and relax. Watch the episode of *Ozark* that Ben and I watched without you because you fell asleep, and you're still butthurt about it."

I scowl at her. "I'm not *butthurt*. You just don't expect your husband and wife to betray you like that."

She laughs. "And then I want you to take a shower, get dressed in those sexy gray sweatpants we all love on you..." Her fingers tap my pectoral muscle. "And I want you to go downstairs."

I give her a bemused look. "Downstairs..."

"Uh-huh," she nods.

The unspoken words between us give me the chills. She bites her lip.

"And you're okay...?" I ask. "Putting Ethan to bed by yourself and everything?"

"I'm supermom, we all know this," she smiles. "But really, I'm exhausted. I'm gonna give him a bath, put him to bed, and then I'm crashing. I'll probably be asleep by the time you're done eating."

I can't help the grin I'm giving her. She's really just the perfect wife, in every single way.

Hovering over her mouth, I whisper, "You know he's gonna keep me down there for hours."

She lets out a soft hum. "Don't make a mess."

I can't help but laugh while I kiss her softly, cherishing the feel of her pouty lips and her sweet floral scent. She's the femininity I love; the contrast to Ben's hard, rough edges.

I love them both so much, it's crazy.

Two hours later, I'm done eating, showered, and dressed in exactly the sweatpants Jess advised. I still haven't even seen Ben since earlier, but now that I know we're having a night alone, that familiar nervous excitement is thrumming in my veins.

It feels just like that first night, when I came down to the basement to find Ben.

My girlfriend's father...

A terrible idea in theory that somehow turned in the best decision I've ever made.

Strutting down the stairs into the dimly lit basement, I look around for my husband. I'd definitely expected him to be on the couch watching TV with a beer...

But he's not.

In fact, I don't see him anywhere.

The unknown is working me up even more, goosebumps sheeting my flesh as I walk to the fridge and grab a beer. Twisting off the top, I take a sip and have a seat on the couch.

Half the beer is gone by the time I turn the TV on, and then the rest of it goes while I surf channels, trying to find something to watch.

Eventually, I settle on some movie, and just as I'm about to get up and go for another beer, I hear footsteps.

"You want another?" Ben's gruff voice comes from the dark, and I turn over the back of the couch to find him sauntering over to the fridge from where his desk is.

"You were down here the whole time?" I ask, my lips curling in amusement.

"I wanted to watch and see if you did anything interesting," he admits teasingly, bringing two bottles over to the couch. He plops down next to me and hands me one. "But you're just a boring old married guy."

Our fingers brush when he hands me the beer, and I swear to God, the fact that it's been two years and his touch still zaps me in the balls is the most mesmerizing thing I've ever experienced.

I bite the inside of my cheek while I watch him, sipping his beer. Plush lips wrapped around the head of the bottle, throat adjusting as he swallows...

I'm still just as fascinated by him as I was that first night, too. Two years, and in fact, I'm even hungrier now.

Sipping from my beer, I lean back on the couch and pretend to watch the movie. "That's me... Just a boring married guy with a baby who restores old cars in his garage." I peek at him. "Pretty clique, huh?"

His sky-blue eyes sparkle at me. "So cliché. I bet you bore your wife in the sack, too."

I can't help the rumbly laugh that bubbles from my throat. "You have no idea."

The tension in the air is building while we sit side-by-side. I couldn't tell you if I tried what's happening in this movie because I'm too busy watching my husband in my peripheral, dressed in sweats like mine and a white t-shirt that hugs his bulk of muscles so well it may as well not even be there, while he sits still and plays this game.

Games with Ben are my favorite pastime, honestly. For someone who claimed to be that boring married guy before we met, he certainly makes everything... thrilling.

Minutes pass, and I can feel Ben inching closer to me. Every time he pretends to stretch, he gets closer, and it reminds me so much of me two years ago, I could implode.

I know he's doing this on purpose. And now I'm anxiously awaiting his next move.

Ben finishes his beer and leans forward to place the bottle on the coffee table. And when he comes back, he's so close that our arms are touching.

I gulp back the rest of my beer, and he reaches for the bottle, taking it from my hand, making sure to really let his fingers linger on mine this time.

My face tilts to his and I watch him watching me, his eyes falling to my lips only briefly. Then he places my bottle down, turning to face me until our knees are touching.

"So... Mr. Lockwood," he rumbles, leaning back on the couch, his fingers ghosting over the nape of my neck. "I have a question for you."

I swallow. "Ask away, Mr. Harper."

His smile goes wicked. "As far as blowjobs go... do you think you can tell the difference between a girl's mouth... and a guy's?" His fingers dance along my nape, playing with my hair.

My cock thumps hard in my pants, my balls yelling at me to tackle him and show him exactly who that mouth belongs to.

But the game...

"I wouldn't know," I mumble, feigning nervousness that's honestly a little bit real. "I've only ever been with girls."

"I see..." he nods. "Well, for the sake of testing the theory..."

And then he slides off the couch onto his knees.

He moves my legs apart, wedging himself in between them while he peers up at me, biting his lip until my cock is leaking in my sweats.

"Fuck..." I whisper, wanting those perfect lips more than I want to breathe.

"Close your eyes," he demands in a soft voice, like a puff of smoke into the air.

I do as he says, forcing them shut, even though I desperately want to watch everything he's doing. He slides his large hands up my thighs, kneading as he goes, then takes the waistband of my pants and pulls them down, my eager dick poking out. I lift my hips so he can get them down more, at which point he rubs my bare thighs with his hands until I can't help but hum.

"That feels good," I whisper without even thinking, and he chuckles.

"*That* feels good? Wow... You're an easy sell, huh?"

"Your hands are so strong," I rasp as he continues to massage my thighs, pushing them apart wider as he does.

"So you can obviously tell I'm a guy..." He mumbles and I nod. "How about now?"

His hand fists around my erection and I whimper.

"Mmm... yea. Yea, that hand is very... masculine."

"But you like it?" His voice is like the purr of a high-horse engine. Growly and rough, but somehow soothing and as smooth as caramel.

I nod slowly. "I never thought I would, but... don't stop."

He hums, giving my cock one long stroke, from my balls all the way up, then back down, tender yet insistent at once.

"Uhh." My hips push forward into his hand.

Then his fingers trail down to my nuts as he caresses them. "You like this too, don't you? Having a guy play with you like this..."

I nod again, faster this time. "Yes. I know I shouldn't want it... but I do."

"I'll give you whatever you want, Mr. Lockwood."

Suddenly I feel him leaning forward, and his warm, wet mouth seals over the head of my cock. I gasp out loud while he sucks me hard then pops off.

"How does that feel?"

"Oh *so good*."

He does it again, sucking on the tip of me like candy, pulling out a pulse of precum that makes my toes curl.

"You're fucking delicious," he growls, then sucks me again, using his tongue to really work up my shaft.

"God fucking damn." I can't help peeking down at him.

And I'm not at all surprised to find him already gazing up

at me, with my hard cock sliding in and out of his perfect mouth.

He pulls off and scolds, "Eyes closed."

Pouting, I close them, catching his grin as I do.

He continues to lick up and down my erection, his warm tongue leaving saliva all over me before he slurps me into his mouth once more, sucking deep, until I hit the back of his throat.

"Fuck *yes*." I reach for his face, holding his jaw while he works me over, in and out, deeper and harder.

When he pulls off again, he rasps, "Can you tell this is a man's mouth sucking the life out of your cock, Mr. Lockwood?"

I hum, shifting my hips up to him again. "Ben, it's you. It's your mouth I want to live in for fucking ever. Nothing has ever felt as good as *you* do."

He pauses for a moment, and I don't give a fuck about the game. I open my eyes to look down at him while he gazes up at me from his knees, wide chest moving with heavy breaths.

"That's exactly how I felt," he whispers. My head cocks. "That first night, two years ago. When you were on your knees where I am right now. I didn't give a flying fuck that you were a man… I just never wanted the feeling to stop."

"Baby," I breathe, and this time we keep our eyes together as he takes me back into his mouth.

Steadily, he works up and down, sucking hard and growling on me, his lashes fluttering when my head pushes into the back of his throat. Holding his jaw, I push myself deeper, and he gags a little, but then he moans on my cock, writhing into me for more.

"You suck so good, Ben Harper," I tell him, fisting his golden hair while he throats my dick until I'm about to burst.

But then he pulls off, eyes sparkling up at me while he breathes heavily.

"I want you to fuck me," he growls. "*Please*, baby."

"Tell me what you want." My fingers brush his jaw and down his throat while he swallows.

"I want you to stuff me with this big dick." He climbs back up onto the couch. I'm immediately reclining so he can straddle me. "I want to look in your eyes while you come so deep inside me it takes days for it all to leak out."

"I fucking love you so much," I whisper, ripping his t-shirt over his head.

"I love you, baby." He yanks my pants off the rest of the way. "Make me naked?"

I grin lazily, shoving his sweatpants down until his massive dick flops out onto mine. He squirms out of them the rest of the way, pressing our heated flesh together. The warmth we make when we're wrapped up like this is so fucking satisfying. I could stay like this forever.

Of course it would never happen like that. We're insatiable, that much is clear.

"Kiss me?" Ben pleads over my mouth, and I grab his jaw in both of my hands, tugging him to me.

He moans when our lips meet, and I swallow it up, desperate for more while we kiss each other stupid. His hands are on my pecs, gripping them hard, my nipples peaked beneath his palms like little pebbles. Our hips move together, rippling like waves while we chase friction, naked and kissing and *fuck* it's all so hot I might burst into flames.

"Sit on my cock, Benjamin," I growl, and he whines, slipping his tongue into my mouth to lap at mine.

Ben is an anomaly, I swear. He has this dominant side to him that gives me chills, but then when we're alone and touching, the sexiest vulnerability shines through, and he becomes putty in my hands. It's just one of the many, many, *many* things I fell in love with about him.

He feeds my every need and then some.

Reaching between the couch cushions, he grabs a small bottle of lube we have stashed there—we have lubed stashed in almost every room of the house, it's ridiculous. *But hey... gotta be prepared at a moment's notice.*

He opens it and squirts some into his hand, rubbing it all over my inches. But before he can reach behind himself, I take the lube and squirt some onto my fingers.

"That's my job," I tell him, watching him tug his lip between his teeth while I move my slick fingers around to the crack of his ass.

Sliding them in between, I swirl lubrication all over his rim while his eyes fall shut. Then I stuff one finger inside, fast, with no warning.

"Mmmfuck," he gasps, head dropping back. "*More.*"

I shove a second finger inside and he's trembling. I can see the chill washing over him, his nipples all bunched up and waiting for my mouth.

"Let me suck your nipples while I finger you, baby."

He moves himself over me so I can lick and suck and bite all over his chest while I give him two more fingers at once. He's mewling like a lion I've tamed into a docile kitten, ass writhing back against my hand while I fuck him with four fingers, in and out, hard, the way he likes it, my mouth devouring his nipples like sweet treats.

He reaches behind himself and grabs my cock, stroking it in his fist until precum is just *leaking* out of me.

"Get on it," I growl, dizzy and vibrating with wanton need. "Get on my dick right now. I want all that cum inside you."

He groans, hoarse and shaky as I pull my fingers out of him and he immediately positions himself over my hips.

Both of our chests are heaving, the sounds of heavy panting ringing through the air as he sits himself down on my cock, welcoming every *single* inch. His eyes flutter shut while he slides down my dick like a pole, taking it all until he's seated on my pelvis, his big dick is flinching on my abs.

I shift my hips and he shudders, precum pulsing out of him onto me. I swipe it with my thumb and reach up, stuffing it into his mouth.

He sucks it off, locking our eyes while he begins to move.

"Mmmm..." He rumbles on my thumb.

I tug it out of his mouth and grin. "What was that?"

"Your dick is so big, baby," he gasps, starting out his riding slow, building a rhythm of his hips to work up and down.

"Yea?" I grip his waist and help him move gradually. "You like having me up in your guts?"

His eyes roll back, and he arches, fucking himself with my dick, finding those good feelings he's chasing while I watch him.

Seeing him like this is my ultimate obsession. Sure, I love fucking Ben, every way I can get him. *On his back, on all fours, on his side with me sort of like... ramming my cock into him while he screams.*

But this... *This*. Having him on top, riding me, is just... It's a sight to behold.

All his muscles constricting everywhere, especially his abs when my dick hits his pleasure spot. The way his eyes roll back and his face gets flushed, his golden hair tousled about and his lip between his teeth...

And best of all, his dick. His big, fat, juicy cock that I love so much, bobbing around while he humps me into oblivion.

I literally have to close my eyes and breathe for a second or I'll come instantly.

"*Fuck me*, Ryan, you feel so good," he groans, gripping my chest with his long fingers while his hips move forward and back, up and down, faster and faster.

"That's it, baby," I croon to him, sliding my hands over his. "Fuck my cock. Ride me hard, Ben."

"Mmm yea... You're fucking... *perfect*."

My heart swells at his words.

"*You're* perfect. Look at you... Like a huge, sexy wet dream come to life. Chase that orgasm, baby. I want to watch your big dick come all over me."

A garbled noise breaks from his lips, his eyelids drooping closed while he goes at it, harder and harder.

"Bounce on this cock, husband." I lift up into him and he gasps.

We're fucking so hard I feel like the couch is falling apart, springs creaking like crazy to mix with the sounds of slapping and grunting... Animal sex music.

"I'm... I'm so..." His voice evaporates as he begins to fall down on me a little.

I reach for his face, holding it while I pump up into his warm, tight hole, using the other hand to grip the meat of his ass cheek.

"Open your eyes, baby," I demand, and he does. "I want you to look into my eyes while you come."

Ben is beyond dazed, and I recognize it. He's about two good thrusts away from exploding everywhere.

And sure enough, he chomps down on his lower lip, forcing himself to keep his eyes open while he whines.

And breaks.

His orgasm shoots all over me, up my chest and onto my neck while Ben's voice snaps from all the heavy panting.

Just seeing him come is enough to push me over the edge. And I palm his ass so hard he'll have bruises, yanking his mouth to mine while I murmur on his lips, "I'm coming with you, baby."

"Come with me... God, *yes*, Ryan, I love you." All of his

words come out as one stream, and I devour them out of his mouth while my cock blows off inside him, shooting pulse after pulse of cum deep in his body.

"I fucking love you more than words," I breathe as the spinning slows.

We suck at each other's lips, tongues tangling in the fervent lust we hold for each other.

The same we've been making since that first night. Right fucking here.

Ben

Ryan and I fell asleep in the basement.

After the intense, animalistic hump-sesh, we were too tired to move, let alone fix ourselves up and go upstairs.

It was romantic, and just the sort of alone time we'd both been craving. Unfortunately, falling asleep in a sea of jizz is never really a good idea. So we're feeling all kinds of icky sticky as we make our ways into the shower.

It's early enough that Jess and Ethan are still asleep, so we're tiptoeing around. And inside the shower, I grab my husband by the waist and just hold onto him.

"You're amazing," I whisper into his neck as the water cascades over us.

"You're a giant teddy bear after you get turned out," he chuckles, and I bite him.

"I'm being serious." I pull away so I can gaze into the moss of his irises. "I really fucking love you. And not just because of your amazing ability to turn me out."

He laughs harder and my grin widens.

"So you're glad you married me, then?" His brow quirks as he lathers shampoo onto his hands and massages it into my hair.

"I wouldn't trade you for anything." My eyes close while he massages my scalp with his strong fingers.

"I was thinking about the wedding, actually," he rumbles, moving my head back, underneath the stream of water to rinse.

Wiping my eyes, I peek at him. "Yea?"

He nods. "About Thailand. And how incredible it was..."

It's funny how as soon as he mentions it, a slideshow of images flick through my mind. All the sun, skin bronzed and glistening, cool water, fresh air, tropical wildlife. The delicious food and even more delicious sex, all over the damn place.

There's no other way to put it. It was heaven on earth.

"We said we'd go back for our anniversary..." Ryan says while washing his hair. I smack his hands away so I can do it, to which he grins.

"Yea. But it wasn't really in the cards last year. We've been so busy..."

"I know. And I'm not complaining," he says as he rinses his hair. "Anniversary one was purely awesome. But I'm just saying... I think we should make more time for trips. Don't you?"

Pressing my lips together so I don't reveal my excitement at the fact that he's *literally* reflecting back my exact thoughts from the last few weeks.

I'm dying to plan another vacation. And honestly, I think I already found the perfect spot. That's what I was actually doing last night in my office. Not working.

Oops.

"Should we take it to the Queen?" I ask him with an eager smirk on my lips.

"Take what to the Queen?" Jessica staggers into the bathroom, tying her blonde locks up in a bun on top of her head.

I give Ryan a look that says, *you go. She never says no to you.*

"We were thinking about planning a vacation..." He mumbles hesitantly, watching Jess through the glass of the shower stall while she brushes her teeth. "I know it'll be hard to leave Ethan at this point, but we've been working so hard lately, don't you think? We deserve some kid-free fun. Plus, there's no shortage of people in our lives eager to watch him for a few days." His eyes flit to mine. "Or maybe a week or... so."

Jessica eyes us in the mirror while she spits out her toothpaste.

"What do you think, love?" I ask her. "You think you could sign off on say... Valentine's Day? Somewhere tropical?"

She turns to face us, popping her hip out and crossing her arms over her chest.

For a second, I'm afraid she's going to shoot this plan right out of the sky like a fighter jet.

But then she blinks and says, "Excuse me... Are you really asking if I'd like to spend Valentine's Day away from my beautiful son whom I love so very much, in a tropical place eating amazing food and banging my gorgeous husbands nonstop?"

Ryan and I share a look while Jess whips the shirt over her head and opens the shower.

He chuckles, "Well, the Queen's in." Then he turns his hungry eyes on me. "Where did you have in mind?"

Two days later, we're hosting game night at our place.

Everyone is due over any minute, and I'm sipping scotch and sending good vibes to my husband and wife while they do everything.

Jess is arranging trays of snacks on the dining room table when the doorbell rings.

"I'll get it!" I shout with a mouthful of a particularly scrumptious coconut shrimp.

"Damn right you will," Ryan chuckles.

Sauntering to the door, I open it with a smile. "Hey! There they are."

All of our friends and family—Greg and Marie, Bill and Rachel, Jacob and Laura, the usual crew—greet me with smiles and a bunch of noise as I welcome them inside.

"Place smells great, Lockwood," Greg pats me on the shoulder.

"Yea, no thanks to him, I bet," Bill teases, and we fake-gut-punch each other.

"My darling brother," Jacob says, giving me a hug.

"Ladies, lovely as ever." I kiss them all on the cheeks, following the sounds of everyone embracing Jess and Ryan.

"Did you invite Tate?" Bill asks, and I don't miss the fact that he's mainly looking at Ryan with this question.

It gives my jaw a little clench.

Jess answers. "We did, but he's working out of town."

"He's actually in Tokyo," Jacob says, stuffing a chip loaded with guacamole into his mouth.

"Tokyo?" Ryan looks surprised as he takes the last bowl from Jess, setting it on the table. "Must be some new account."

"You mean he didn't share the details with you?" Bill asks. "I heard you two talk all the time." He glances at me and smirks.

"You're highly annoying," I roll my eyes.

"Yea, we *all* try to keep in touch, not just me and Tate," Ryan says. "In fact, I have to drive up to ABQ next weekend to help Alec and Kayla with wedding stuff."

"Oh yea? When are they getting married?" Jacob asks.

"April," Ryan says with a beaming smile. It's fully adorable how excited he is to be Alec's best man.

"Speaking of travel," I use this as my segue, and excuse to get right down to the point. Everyone looks my way, minus Greg who's still eating, as usual. "We're going on vacation for Valentine's Day. So we need volunteers to watch Ethan for ten days."

"Ten days?!" Multiple people squawk at once.

"You're really okay to leave Ethan for that long?" Jess's sister asks her.

Jess looks worried. "If I say *yes* too enthusiastically, does that make me a bad mother?"

Rachel and Laura laugh.

"Look, we really need this vacation," I tell them, sipping my drink.

"Oh yea, your life seems really tough, Lockwood," Greg mumbles sarcastically. "Great job, adorable kid and two partners to share it all with. Boo freaking hoo."

I can't help the deranged look of amusement I'm giving him.

"Are you saying you'd rather have *two* partners?" Marie folds her arms and glares at him.

He has this dopey look on his face, like a dog that just got caught eating the Easter ham.

"Wait a minute. Is that why you agreed to host game night?" Bill accuses. "So you can butter us up to take care of your kid while you flit off to some island somewhere?"

I shrug. "Yea, kind of."

"*No*, it's not." Ryan elbows me.

"Plus, look how many of you there are!" Jess adds. "You can each split him for three days."

"He's not a timeshare, babe," Ryan chuckles, and she gives him a look.

"Don't be silly, we don't mind watching him," Laura says with a smile. "He's the easiest baby in the world, anyway."

"Yea, I mean where is he right now? You'd have no idea he's even here," Rachel adds.

"Don't jinx it, please," Jess sighs.

Bill picks up a rolled taquito and bites into it. "So, where you crazy kids off to this time?"

Jess and Ryan share an excited look. "Well, you might realize we're having all Mexican themed snacks tonight..."

"You're going to Cabo?!" Rachel gasps.

"No. Better." Ryan is nearly squealing.

Everyone looks at me for some reason. So I tell them, "Tulum."

Jacob and Laura make a sort of *ooh* and *aah*. But the others look confused.

"*Tulum*? That's in Mexico?" Greg mumbles while chewing.

I nod.

"Oh yea, I've heard of it," Bill says. "A little extravagant, don't ya think?" He slaps me on the back.

"Nothing is too luxurious for my King and Queen." I grin at Ryan and Jess and they both bite their lips.

"Aww," Rachel swoons.

"That doesn't make sense," Bill retorts. "If they're the King and Queen, then who are you?"

"I don't know, we're all knights," I grumble. "Who cares? I'm trying to tell you about the trip."

"Valentine's Day is only a few weeks away!" Laura squeals. "That's so exciting. Where are you staying?"

"This amazing little resort right on the water," Jess says, pouring some wine.

"It's called Abre Tus Ojos," Ryan announces through an unwavering grin.

Greg's brows zip. "Eat your eyes?"

"*Open* your eyes," I scoff. "Jesus, we live in New Mexico."

"And what exactly are you love birds going to get up to in Tulum for ten days?" Rachel asks, smirking.

I share a look with my husband and wife, the three of us quaking with excitement.

The possibilities are *endless*.

Stay tuned for the next chapter of **The Vacation!**

Sign up for the Flipping Hot Newsletter to stay updated!

A QUICK NOTE

I just wanted to say thank you to everyone who read the novella last summer when it was free. And also to everyone who didn't, and then proceeded to ask me about it constantly. You really lit a fire under my ass. If it weren't for you all, I might not have made this happen, so really... Thank you.

You'll probably notice that there's a big difference between the first three bonus scenes and the Pride novella. Well, that's because I wrote the bonus scenes right after I published PUSH in 2019. And I wrote PULL last year. There is a *monumental* difference in my writing from then to now, and so I also want to thank my loyal readers, who started with PUSH way back when, and followed me along in this crazy, incredible journey.

I have learned so much over the course of this publishing adventure. Not even just about my writing, but myself. That is why coming back to Ben, Ryan, and Jessica after two years was so important to me. It felt like a reunion of sorts.

Like I was coming *home*.

Every single bit of these three sits permanently fixed in my heart. They really were the start of Nyla K, and I greatly look forward to everything else the future brings for them.

And I know you will, too!

That means they're not done... Hence, Tulum. ;)

A QUICK NOTE

If you don't get the Tulum reference, read Distorted right away.

Lastly, please do me the hugest favor and leave a review! I know some people tried when I released PULL for free last summer, but if you could do so again on the official Goodreads page, and on Amazon, it would be so incredibly helpful to me!

Love you all.

ALSO FROM NYLA K.

Thank you for reading

Flipping Hot Fiction by Nyla K

The Midnight City Series:

Andrew & Tessa's Trilogy

(Forbidden/Age Gap, celebrity romance, suspense. Read in order)

Midnight City (TMCS #1)

Never Let Me Go (TMCS #2)

Always Yours (TMCS #3)

Alex & Noah

Seek Me (TMCS #4 – Standalone, Friends to lovers/Angst)

Unexpected Forbidden Romance:

PUSH (Standalone, Taboo/MMF)

To Burn In Brutal Rapture (Standalone, Taboo/Age Gap)

Double-edged (Standalone, Taboo/MMM) Coming March 10th, 2022!

Alabaster Penitentiary:

Distorted, Volume 1 (MM)

Joyless, Volume 2 (MMF)

Brainwashed, Volume 3 (MM) – Coming in 2022!

Fragments, Volume 4 (MM)

Ivory, Volume 5 (mystery, *wink wink*)

Twisted Tales Collection:

Serpent In White (A polyamorous, MMM cult retelling of *The White Snake*)

Twisted Christmas: A Taboo Christmas Anthology

Unwrap Him by Nyla K (An Age Gap, Taboo MM) Coming back Christmas, 2022!

Don't forget to share and leave a review! It means the world!

ABOUT THE AUTHOR

Hi, guys! I'm Nyla K, otherwise known as Nylah Kourieh; an awkward sailor-mouthed lover of all things romance, existing in the Dirty Lew, up in Maine, with my fiancé, who you can call PB, or Patty Banga if you're nasty. When I'm not writing and reading sexy books, I'm rocking out to Machine Gun Kelly and YUNGBLUD, cooking yummy food and fussing over my kitten (and no, that's not a euphemism). Did I mention I have a dirtier mind than probably everyone you know?

I like to admire hot guys (don't we all?) and book boyfriends, cake and ice cream are my kryptonite. I can recite every word that was ever uttered on *Friends*, *Family Guy*, and *How I Met Your Mother*, red Gatorade is my lifeblood, and I love to sing, although I've been told I do it in a Cher voice for some reason. I'm very passionate about the things that matter to me, and art is probably the biggest one. If you tell me you like my books, I'll give you whatever you want. I consider my readers are my friends, and I welcome anyone to find me on social media any time you want to talk books or sexy dudes!

Get at me:

AuthorNylaK@gmail.com, or my PA
amberbookobsession@gmail.com

Sign up for the Flipping Hot Newsletter for exclusive content!

Join my reader group! Nyla K's Flipping Hot Readers!

Happy reading!

facebook.com/authorNylaK
twitter.com/MissNylah
instagram.com/Authornylak
tiktok.com/@authornylak
goodreads.com/authornylak
bookbub.com/profile/nyla-k

Made in United States
Orlando, FL
31 March 2024